Ethiopian Woman

JACK REYNOLDS

PUBLISHED BY FIDELI PUBLISHING, INC.

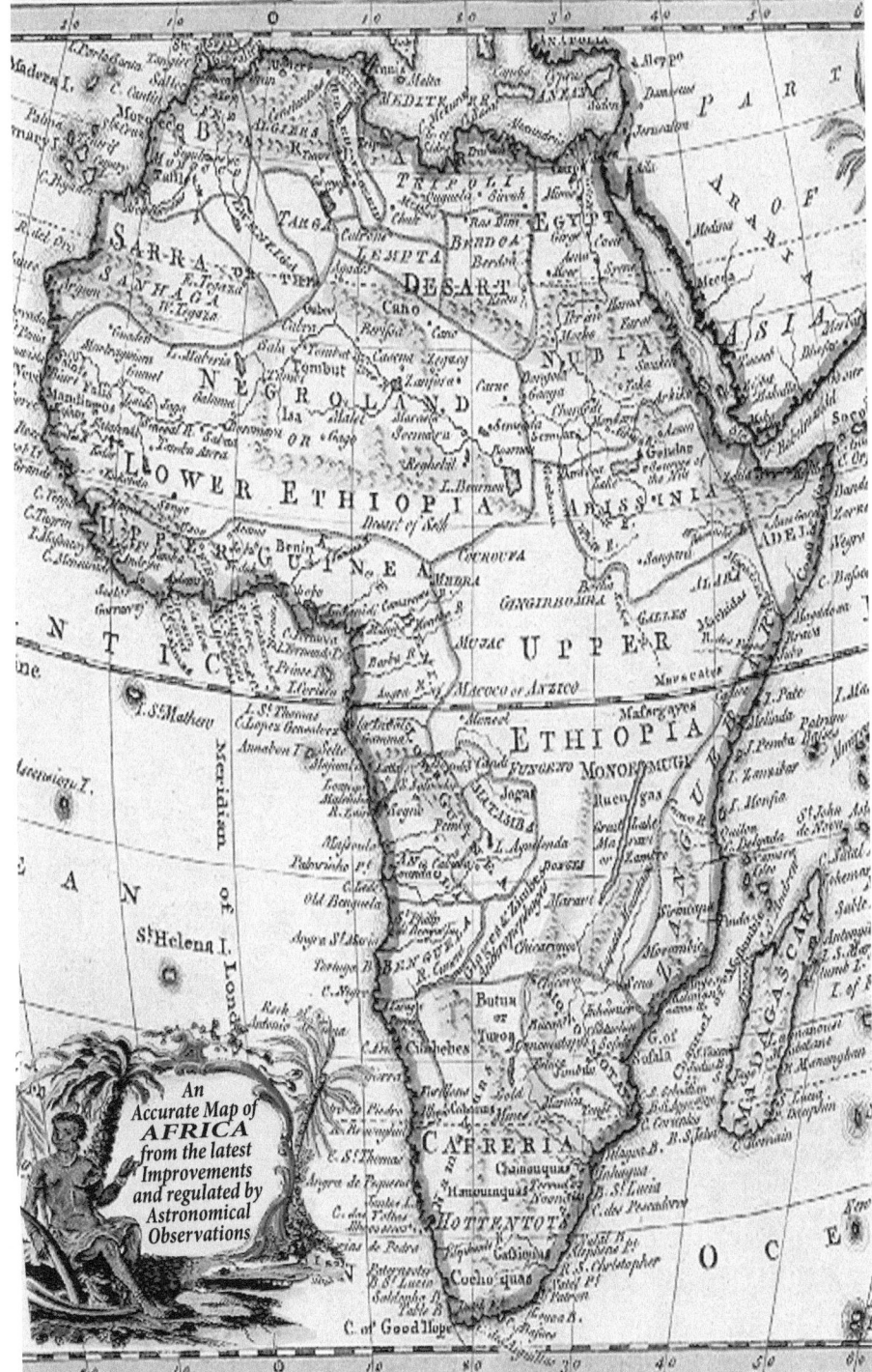

An
Accurate Map of
AFRICA
from the latest
Improvements
and regulated by
Astronomical
Observations

Dedication

Thoughts ... are the seeds of reality.

There are spiritual rewards for those who look closely at the truths. There is hopelessness in store for those who accept the truth without doubt.

He... was told that a torch is hot and he would not rest his hand upon it. She... desires to touch the flame and knows what is hot. Here... is born curiosity. Here... dies blind compliance.

There is a time to believe and a time to question every truth. There is a time to follow and a time to lead.

From the minds of men was born Almighty God. From the womb of God was born all of mankind...

This story is dedicated to all of the "daughters of men" who have inspired the "Sons of God" to stand upright and question every wrong ... be they committed by man, angel or God ... Here's to those who will not justify wrong, even for the Almighty.

> *"And the sons of God began to look upon the daughters of men and saw that they were beautiful."* (GENESIS 6:2)

Author's Note

This story is based on the life of an Ethiopian woman that existed in the Holy Bible as the wife of Moses (Numbers 12 V-I). "Miriam" (the sister of Moses and Aaron) "and Aaron began to talk against Moses because of his Kushite wife." The Kushite woman, according to the James Hasting Dictionary of the Bible, refers to Ethiopian woman: Cush; refers to Ethiopia.

"Cush" in the Old Testaments designated Ethiopian and is the only name used there for that region. It is the same as the Egyptian Kosh. Broadly speaking, it answers to the modem Nubian. More specifically, the Egyptian Kosh extended southwards from the first Cararact at Syene and embraced Sudan. Kush was a rich source of gold. It attracted the lucrative caravan trade of Egypt from early times. Kush was conquered and annexed by Egypt under the 12th Dynasty (199-1786 BC). After the decline of the 22nd Libyan Dynasty, the Kushites became powerful and gradually encroached Northern Egypt. So at length, an Ethiopian Dynasty was established 715-656 BC, which was later over thrown by the Assyrians. History tells us that Ethiopia is a translation of the Hebrew Cush, which is derived from Kosh, the Egyptian name of Nubia.

For he (Moses) had married a Kushite. "Has the Lord spoken only through Moses?" they asked "Hasn't he also spoken through us?" And the Lord heard this.

Now Moses was a very humble man, more humble than anyone else on the face of the earth.

At once the Lord said to Moses, Aaron and Miriam. "Come out to the tent of meetings all three of you." So the three of them came out. Then the Lord came down in a pillar of cloud. He stood at the entrance of the tent and summoned Aaron and Miriam. When both of them stepped forward, he said. "Listen to my words.

When a prophet of the Lord is among you. I reveal myself to him in visions. I speak with him in dreams. But this is not true of my servant Moses; he is faithful in all my house. With him I speak face to face, clearly and not in riddles; he sees the form of the Lord. Why then were you not afraid to speak against my servant Moses?" (Numbers 12, V. l thru 8).

Following these biblical verses the Lord became furious toward Miriam and Aaron to the point where he stricken Miriam with leprosy and she turned "like snow." Aaron begged Moses not to let her flesh be eaten away. After he had seen his sister, Moses asked God to please heal her. God would not let her go unpunished not even for Moses.

With such a powerful tum of events and knowing the importance of Miriam and Aaron; it only stands to reason that God felt strongly toward this Ethiopian woman, to the point that he was inclined to put the sister of Moses to death. Miriam's acts probably constitute the first act of racism, based upon not only the color of her skin but also her assumption that the choice of Moses (probably inspired by God himself) was not acceptable to the Levite woman.

This section of the bible (Numbers) like most writings of Moses were intended to record the history of the twelve tribes of Israel or the twelve sons of Jacob, their forefathers (starting with the generation of Noah) and the descendants of each tribe before and after the Exodus. So it stands to reason that Moses may have omitted his relationship with his Ethiopian wife because she was not a descendant of Jacob or an Israelite in search of the promise land. He may have concluded that she nor his children by her were relevant to the history of the tribes of Abraham, Isaac or Jacob, (who was the father of the twelve to whom God had made his promises) who is also known as Israel. In this writer's mind, Mericah (a fictitious name given to the second wife of Moses) would stand as an essential beginning to the tribe of Moses and more importantly the ancestors of many of today's African Americans, who have been deprived of direct linkage to being the children of God via the biblical heritage that so many other nationalities claim. With just the short mention that she, Mericah, existed, it can be easily concluded that she probably bore his children, due to the consummation of marriage being sexual throughout the scriptures and the importance of direct descendants and their inheritance are bases of being able to claim a share of eternity that is proclaimed by other Hebrew descendants. This would give the Ethiopians a kinship to holiness.

The claim by many that people of African descent were just objects of slavery has historically been supported by European novelist and others through the ages. They categorically have written out Africans and their biblical importance. By definition, for example; when most people of today are asked to define what exactly is their perception of a biblical slave or a slave designated by a curse of God, it is concluded that they are black and of African descent. When in actuality most slaves were of non-African descent and were generally captives of wars.

Other deceptive writings and theatrical impressions, such as a white Cleopatra, Jesus with blue eyes and blond hair or a Moses that resembles Charlton Heston or even the non acknowledgment that the Kushites or Cushites actually ruled a large portion of the biblical world for hundreds of years including areas now known as Greece, Turkey, Iraq, Italy and especially Egypt, have taken away the roles that people of color have played in the development of laws and key achievements in humanitarian ways of governing and even the steering of the world to the acceptance of the concept of one God.

By definition, if you are black you have no place in biblical writings unless you were a servant of some sort. In reality the Africans were respected as being well advanced in the medical, architectural, spiritual and political achievements.

Mericah is a fictitious character and is not intended to conflict with actual biblical or historical writings. She was born into the biblical environment to open minds to the possibility of what may have been. Additionally, she may inspire other storytellers to bring to life strong characters with morals and meaningfulness designed to change the image of a race of people who are cursed by definition.

Chapter 1

S he peered through a small opening on the inner courtyard side of the Pharaohs Palace. This was home for all of the concubines, virgin wives and female captives of the Pharaoh.

Thousands of Hebrews and other slaves from all over the region were celebrating jubilantly as far as her eyes could see. "Thanks to God of Moses we are 'free at last' ... all praise to the Great One ... all praise to the God of Abraham, Isaac and Jacob," they proclaimed loudly and repeatedly.

Herds of sheep, goats and fowl were peppered among the crowds as cymbals clanged and children ran about merrily chasing and jumping with glee as if they knew the meaning of this great exodus. The Pharaohs ground army and horsemen were standing high on the public mounds of stones along all the marked pathways that divided the Hebrews and slave quarters from the Egyptians and allies of the Pharaoh. They stood proud and arrogant ready to put the Hebrews to death at the command of their officers. Yet, the people had no fear, the spirit of God had filled their hearts with the desire to fulfill the prophecy and the courage to shout with joy without fear of retribution. The slaves were confident that they would now live under the glory of God in the land of milk and honey, the promise land of Abraham, the God given land of Isaac also known as Israel.

"Why are the Hebrews shouting?" Mericah asked or perhaps thought out loud, since the question was directed to no one because no one among the Hebrews would have known the answer.

The Pharaoh's den of women was off limits to the common folks and men of all walks of life. They were the pride of the Pharaoh pure untouched and destined to be placed by the Pharaoh as wives and servants of royalty. Or if they were of royalty to have the honor of reaching everlasting life with the Pharaoh as he moved from this world to the next into the burial chambers of the kings.

Mericah had been chosen. She was to be placed, as a wife to the Pharaoh, in his tomb to enjoy his presence in all eternity. She was born of royalty in her own land of Ethiopia, of which she has little memory. Mericah had been taken from her father, in a battle for the lives of her people, during a conflict with the Pharaoh's army long before she turned her present age of sixteen.

As a chosen, she had her own Hebrew and Ethiopian maidservants. Daily, she was anointed and beautified with the perfumes, oils, eye and lip colors of her Cushite homeland. Her beauty was known throughout the lands of Egypt. Few men had ever laid eyes upon her.

Yet the word of her beauty had spread, perhaps by the servants or perhaps by the gods; as it was thought that she was born a princess and would someday become a goddess. In any event, she would stay a virgin and enter the next world as such.

She recognized her destiny and was not only eloquent but proud and looked forward to her ultimate crown among the gods.

"What is happening?" again her question went unanswered by all that had now gathered to watch the spectacle of thousands leaving Egypt.

Suddenly the great doors of the chamber of virgins burst open and the pharaoh's priest entered and declared. "All who are Hebrew and descendants of the tribes of Rueben, Simeon, Levi, Judah, Issachar, Zebulun, Joseph, Benjamin, Dan, Naphtali, Asheri and Gad, stand forward and prepare to join the exodus of the Hebrews, for you have been given by the pharaoh to Moses and his GOD. Leave us that we may live without the plagues of Moses. Rapidly, leave this chamber and may the gods be with you."

The virgins did not move. They feared for their lives, for they had not heard of this man called Moses. They moved instead backwards, hiding where they could, afraid of this command. Most had never heard of these tribes and those that had, only remembered a life of submissiveness and servitude to their own tribe. After all, they were all special and served by slaves in preparation for a life in the heavens. Again, the priest shouted, "step forth and leave us in peace." Yet, the center of the chamber remained empty as the virgins backed even closer to the outer walls of the rooms. "No, we are the property of our pharaoh and should not be exposed to the peasants of Moses and his people," said Mericah in a sassy voice.

The chambers became quiet and a mysterious hush fell upon the virgins as they all refuse to leave what had become the only home they knew.

It is said that an angel of the God of Abraham had entered the spirits of his descendants and through out the room the virgins began to yield. One after another they began to release their fears and feel the spirit of God. One after another they came from behind pillars and fixtures to take their places among the Israelites. Without words, they exited no longer worried about the tempting of men or the unknown journey ahead.

Again from the hush came the voice of Mericah "No," she said.

"I am a Cushite, not a Hebrew. I am not a descendant of these tribes nor do I know this God of Moses. I will not be defiled against the will of my destiny, nor will I leave the pharaoh for the journey of which my servants cannot go. For the pharaohs will go and slay my father saying he has taken back his word and thus voiding the treaty with my people. No! I will not go. Leave me to serve my god and the gods of the pharaoh."

In the quiet of the room an angel of God spoke "the choice is not yours for you are right. You are not a descendant of Abraham but a descendant of the fathers of Abraham and the men of God."

3

Mericah was high spirited and still filled with resistance, she would not yield to even an angel of God.

The priest interrupted, "She should surely not be forced to go."

She and her race are the pride of the pharaoh. They are the elite guards of the palace. They are trusted and known to give up their lives for the leadership and their superiors. Again I say surely God would not want those of this black race among the children of Israel."

The angel of God was silent as some of the slaves continued to file one after another through the great doors into the crowds of Hebrews below. The priest went back into the presence of the Pharaoh to inform him that the Cushites were being taken along with the Hebrews.

The Pharaoh was outraged and demanded the presence of Moses and Moses was brought forth.

He asked, "Why do you choose to continue to anger me and trial Egypt and her ways? Does your GOD wish to take the people of Egypt who are not of the tribes of Abraham, but of the Ethiopians; who do not worship your GOD or the GOD of Abraham, Isaac or Jacob? Must we again compare the strengths of our gods against yours for the sake of a black woman and her tribesmen?"

Without response Moses turned and walked away from the Pharaoh and his priest.

"What does this mean?" asked one of the priests. A Hebrew that had entered at the side of Moses responded, "the GOD of Abraham will prevail, we have no say in this matter." With that, Moses and his servants left the presence of the Pharaoh.

Thousands had now exited Egypt. They continued to pour out from the fields and the riverbanks of the Nile. The Pharaoh's army still held fast, in awe of the Pharaoh's decision to let the people of Israel leave. Their swords and spears were eager to put an end to the Israelites. At the Pharaohs command, the armies of Egypt could destroy the unarmed thousands and teach these ingrates the consequences of disobedience and uprising against the gods. Still they held their positions as spectators.

Mericah, was now pacing the chamber floor in front of the remaining virgins, who were watching. She is just a child in the eyes of many and yet her aura of dignity and beauty demanded the respect of all the others.

The chamber doors again burst open. This time four Ethiopian Egyptian guards entered. "Which of you is the daughter of Hameron of Ethiopia?"

"It is I," answered Mericah. "Your father has sent word that you are to leave this place for Moses has brought a curse to the Egyptians. Our armies have gathered in Ethiopia to defend its land and the people of the upper Niie. The Nubians and Cushites demand the return of the daughter of Hameron."

It is written that one day Egypt will again belong to Ethiopia and the gods have recognized that the daughter of Hameron will be the Queen of the Cushites.

In the land of the Ethiopians, women of royalty were extremely important. The mothers of kings actually controlled the nations within and were able to communicate with the gods, just as prophets of the Israelites.

It is written that the Cushites are direct descendants of Cush, the fIrst born son of HAM who was the youngest son of NOAH, whom looked upon Noah's drunken nakedness.

The young princess spoke again; this time softer, this time exposing her youth, this time unsure of herself.

"I must serve the Pharaoh, we must serve the Pharaoh, we are not," she paused and took a deep breath. "I am not a Hebrew. "Am I?"

The guard bowed his head as if ashamed to respond and said, "I am only alive to serve the gods and our nation, being given the choice of serving the Egyptians or living free among the Israelites has caused division among our legend. I have seen the power of the Hebrew GOD of one called Abraham. He has given the Israelites authority over the nature of things. No, we are not Israelites but neither are we Egyptians. We are Ethiopian. But, we are just as much captive as the people of Israel. We have slaved long and fought hard for the Pharaoh and many of us have forgotten our homeland. Now, we have been called to rise up and leave this place. If we stay who will protect us from the Pharaoh when the plagues have stopped? When the Israelites are gone the burden of the common slaves will lie upon the Cushites and captives from southern Canaan. Our status will become the lowest of low. Let us leave this place while the Pharaoh is still under the curse of this GOD."

"What will the gods do to us, if we leave?" she asked.

"The GOD of Israel has put down the gods. They too are powerless in the presence of the GOD of Israel. … Why are you resisting the will of this All Mighty GOD?" asked the guard. "When so many will not leave without you."

The spirit of GOD again entered the chamber of virgins and all could hear a voice that stunned the pit of their hearts.

"Cushite child, your destiny is no longer to serve the gods of your father nor the gods of Egypt. For GOD has found purpose for your people. Rise up and leave this place."

Mericah gazed around the chamber looking for the source of this powerful voice and spoke again with question and courage.

"How can I obey a voice which seems to come from within my own ears and yet all who are here are able to listen."

"God has answered the prayers of your forefathers through this very same voice that you question."

Again the voice said, "Rise up and leave this place." The guards and remaining Cushite virgins had fallen down hiding their faces in fear.

"Show yourself," said Mericah as she alone still remained standing.

"For we all have voices. Whose voice do we hear? Are you Baal? If you are a god take us with you now to paradise and we will serve you as you have never been served before."

After a few moments of silence, Mericah spoke again. "I cannot abandon all that I have been taught, for there are many gods who have many voices. Which god are you? Why is your presence so strongly felt?"

"I am the voice of the GOD of Israel."

"I am the voice of the GOD of many Cushite generations before you. There is no other voice but mine that can reach the ears of the righteous. Now the choice of your people to stay in Egypt is yours and yours alone."

"Will you give Egypt into the hands of the Cushites, if we serve you?" she asked.

There was no answer.

After a long pause "No!" she said, I will not leave Egypt."

"Egypt will be delivered into the hands of the Cushite" the voice said.

The guards began to lift their heads from the floor just enough to see if the young black woman had gone mad. They wondered, who are we to bargain with such a powerful presence?

"Rise up" she said. "We are leaving to join this Moses and may the gods be with us."

Chapter 2

The Cushite virgins were filled with excitement. For not all had accepted the destiny of the tombs of the pyramid as a living servant among the dead.

They began to quickly gather their belongings of clothing, perfumes and spices for the exodus was nearly complete in this part of Egypt.

The Ethiopian guards waited impatiently to escort Mericah and her now followers to the outer courtyard and hopefully into the still vast number of Israelites. Hoping that they too would go unnoticed. They had discarded their armor and now were scantly dressed in their waist high under garments made of linens. The men towered high over the women as they mingled into the crowds. Not long into the journey a soldier of the pharaoh spotted the black men as they past a checkpoint that had been established by the army.

"You," he said, pointing at the huge black Ethiopian who was leading and making an open path for the slave women. "You are not Hebrew," he said, gesturing for additional soldiers to come and assist. "Stop there!"

The Egyptians approached the now unarmed Ethiopian men.

Just then, Mericah stepped between them and proclaimed, "They are my servants. We have been declared along with the Hebrews as freed from the Pharaoh's bondage."

"We have no word of the freedom of Ethiopians. Step to the side," he said.

"Who is your owner?" the guard asked as he spotted the crescent of the pharaoh burned on Mericah's hand. He seemed reluctant to lay eyes upon her, for he realized she was the virgin property of the most high. By now six other soldiers had arrived, one of them the high-ranking commander of the chariots.

"This black woman is claiming the Pharaoh freed her. She wears the mark of the pharaoh's virgins," he said to the ranking officer as he came closer.

Out of the crowd, four more Ethiopian uniformed soldiers stepped closer to Mericah. The Egyptian officer now stood before her and said, "You are a beauty. If the pharaoh doesn't want you, I certainly do." He put his hand upon Mericah's shoulders and pulled her closer as if to look directly into her eyes.

Just as he pulled her shoulders towards him, both of his arms were suddenly cut off at the elbow by an Ethiopian's sword. Within seconds a second blow was struck and the head of the officer fell forward and dropped to the feet of the black princess. Without a word, the Ethiopians slew the rest of the Egyptian soldiers.

"No one is to touch her!" he said as he struck a final blow that cut another Egyptian completely in half at the waist. These were Egyptian trained Ethiopians, the most elite of the Pharaoh's army. They were the kings personal and most trusted guards, yet they did not hesitate to obey the word from their homeland to protect the princess at all cost.

The time was at hand to bring her home, ror she will fulfill the prophecy of her ancestors. She will bear a child who will be the father of sons, who will drive the northern invaders out of Africa forever. It will not be the child of a pharaoh, but a child of the descendants of Cush.

Mericah, for the first time had witnessed the shedding of blood. She began to run back toward the palace as one of the Ethiopian soldiers named Mohab ran in front of her and stood blocking her way without touching her.

"Please stop," he said. "Think of your father and the dreams of your nation. Without you, our time will not begin. Our blood will not carry the blood of God. Our people will not know the joy of warmth and compassion. We will never be given our place in the Heavens."

Mericah stopped, frantically trying to wipe the blood of the soldiers off of her black skin.

She asked, "Who are you?"

"I am Mohad, I am your oldest brother. I have come to take you home"

Mericah began to regain her composure. She looked back toward the crowd of IHebrews, still making their way out of the city. She looked at thirty to forty Ethiopian virgins from her palace chamber, who were staring at her waiting for her to lead them.

She looked at the Ethiopian soldiers, who now numbered into the hundreds, pushing women, children and livestock into the tail end of the crowd of Israelites.

The Egyptian soldiers overseeing the Exodus seemed to be dazed and standing motionless gazing into the heavens. She looked up into the heavens, directly into the eyes of God. She then fell to her knees crying loudly, "My God! My God! I am no one; please do not place this burden upon me, for I am truly a child. I have no knowledge of your ways." The spirit of God had touched her.

"Raise up! Raise yourself up and leave this place; for God has found favor in you and your people. Follow the tribes of Israel until your way is shown to you."

Mericah immediately got up on her feet and looked into the eyes of her brother. Neither he nor any of the others had heard the voice, nor had they seen the light from above.

"Let us obey this God of Abraham. Let us go home." With these words she mounted a nearby ass and joined the Exodus to the Promised Land. She and her people, now numbering into the thousands and growing, prepared to leave.

Chapter 3

As the mass of people approached the western shore of the Red Sea, the Ethiopians were still in the last sector of the Israelite's Exodus. They were familiar with the trade routes to their homeland and reasoned that Moses would have gone northeast out of Egypt, if his intentions were to enter into Canaan.

With the Red Sea east of the camp, they could only be heading south toward the upper Nile region. There was doubt that Moses had the expertise to build enough ships to cross the Red Sea and go into the desert toward Babylon.

With another night upon them, the Ethiopians halted and bedded down as best they could.

Mohab choose forty of is most dependable horsemen and divided them into groups of ten. He stationed each sentry group a three-hour journey apart and behind the last of the clan. Each day one soldier from each group would stay behind and one sent forward as a way to be forewarned of any movement or pursuit by the pharaoh's army.

Mohab did not believe the pharaoh would actually let the Israelites leave. Mohab's premonitions were correct but for a different reason.

Chapter 4

When the Pharaoh got word from his priest traveling with Moses that not only had the pharaoh's elite Ethiopian infantrymen and guards joined the exodus, but the royal virgins and concubines had also left, his anger was rekindled.

In a fit of rage he demanded that they be returned and Moses and the Israelites destroyed. The priest called upon the gods to deliver the tribes of the Israelites into the hands of the Egyptian soldiers. They wanted to get revenge and to bring the body of Moses and his God before the Pharaoh's court.

The chariots of the Pharaoh were immediately gathered and sent to bring back the virgins, especially the Ethiopian princess.

> "The Lord hardened the heart of pharaoh king of Egypt, so that he pursued the Israelites, who were marching out boldly. The Egyptians all pharaoh's horses and chariots pursued the Israelites and overlook them as they camped by the sea near Pi Hahiroth, opposite Baal Zephow."
>
> (Exodus 14-8&9)

Mohab was awakened by one of his centurion horsemen, who frantically proclaimed, "The Pharoah's chariots have been spotted by the last outpost. There are more than a thousand of them and the Pharaoh's army is not far behind."

"How far away are they?" asked Mohab.

"They are four stations behind, not more than one day's journey," the soldier replied.

Mohab went immediately to the tent where Merich the virgins were staying. He paused then announced himself with a sense of urgency. He did not want to panic the women. "The Pharaoh has gathered his army and they are pursuing us with a vengeance. They're not more than one day's journey away from us," he said.

"Can the Israelites defeat them?" Merich asked. She was surprisingly calm under the circumstances. "Do the Israelites know they are coming?"

Mohab answered the last question first. "No, my own sentry just brought me this news. With the God of Abraham and His power I've seen back in Egypt, no one can defeat Moses. I just don't know that the God of the Israelites is aware of the armies of Egypt The Israelites have no weapons and have fought no battles."

"Send someone to Moses and tell him about the Egyptian army," Merich instructed her older brother.

"How far away are the armies of our father?" she asked.

"The core of the Ethiopian army is more than a month's journey away, Even if they could get here, they would be no match for the Egyptians. They are not prepared for a battle against Egypt," was Mohab's response.

At the break of dawn, Merich could see thousands of Israelites. The Mighty Red Sea seemed to be looming just ahead, blocking everything in the direction that they were headed.

Mohab had assembled his force of soldiers and strategically stationed his men to possibly slow down the Pharaoh's chariot force until Merich and the rest of the Ethiopians hide themselves in the crowd of Israelites.

Through that day and into the night, the Ethiopian soldiers slowly moved back until they were about two hours behind the Exodus, still heading directly toward the sea.

By midday of the following day, the dust of the Pharaoh's army could be seen in the far distance. They were approaching at the charging pace of the chariots. They would overcome the end of the Israelite's group before nightfall.

With the backs of his soldiers now in sight, Mohab and the crowds were at a stand still against the sea. Mohab encouraged Mericah to leave, saying, "Moses did not turn south into the flats of the sea of reeds and now we have trapped ourselves against the Red Sea. We must put distance between us and the Israelites; the crowd is moving too slowly. The horsemen can carry you and the Ethiopian women and children back toward the chariots, then turn south and head into the marshes of the Nile. Surely the army will not pursue your small group," he added.

"No," said Mericah. "The chariots will overtake and murder us. At this point Moses will turn and fight. I'm sure he has some plan to protect his people," she continued.

"We have heard that Moses is not with the Israelites. Instead, he and his brother Aaron are in prayer on the shore, north of the crowd." Mohab said.

"Then we must turn and fight with all our might. The gods will hide us from the Egyptian archers," said Mericah to her brother and his officers.

As the Ethiopian soldiers prepared for battle, the crowd began to move. Suddenly, the ground beneath their feet trembled like nothing they had felt before.

Chapter 5

They feel earth rumble, and heard a sound like all the pyramids of Egypt were raining down from the heavens. The air was filled with moisture, yet the skies held no rain. Suddenly, the ground dropped off as the pace of the crowd was increased. The Egyptian chariots were in full charge, coming toward the Israelites.

The pounding of the hooves of the hundreds of horses were drowned out by the roar of the sea as it lifted from its bed. Down and down between the wall of waters the Israelites continued their trek. The ground shook violently beneath their feet and the walls of water on both sides hovered high above their heads. Blindly, they pushed ahead. A heavy mist of seawater and sand swirled above, as if caught in a whirlwind.

The Ethiopians and their soldiers, positioned at the rear of the crowd, began to run as fast as they could. Blindly, the masses moved through the knee-deep sea water. Down and down they went, lower and lower into the d belly of the Red Sea, gasping for air as the moisture became so thick it was like breathing water. Frightened beyond description, they move forward following in the person in front of them.

The last of the Ethiopians backed into the sea, arms raised and ready for battle, just as the first of the chariots came to the seashore and stopped. They were amazed by the powers of this God of Moses and faltered in their quest.

The chariots behind them were still rushing forward in full stride. They had no knowledge of the dividing of the sea. When they reached the beach, they were possessed by the powers of God and could not stop.

As the Ethiopians continued walking forward, the grade of the sea bottom finally began to turn upward, making the struggle even harder. Each step was like lifting fifty-pound weights. Yet they climbed on, realizing that the Pharaoh in his wrath would surely put them to death without mercy.

When the Israelites lost their footing, the Ethiopian soldiers were there to lift them up. The courage and unexplained strength went unquestioned. The crowed bravely continued walking upward and left not one soul behind. After what seemed like an eternity, they reached the eastern shore of the sea. The morning air was still thick, and dawn was approaching.

Finally, when they'd made the crossing, they lay on the ground looking back into the valley of swirling mist and water. Exhausted and helpless, they knelt down by the thousands to pray to the God of Abraham. The Egyptians were still coming fast, filled with hatred and swords drawn for a merciless kill. They thought this violence necessary because their pharaoh demanded it, claiming it was the wish of their gods.

In a last effort, the Ethiopian soldiers got up' an unknown source of strength had suddenly filled their bodies. One after the other, they stood and moved shoulder to shoulder. They jostled to be the first to kill and die

Suddenly, Moses appeared. This was the first time the Ethiopians had seen the savior of the Israelites. His stance was unimpressive, as he stretched out his hand and looked to the heavens. Without a word his eyes slowly looked toward the valley in the sea.

Moses stretched out his hand toward the sea, and all the Lord drove the sea back with a strong eastern wind that turned sea to dry land. The waters were divided so the Israelites could cross the sea walking on dry ground bordered by a wall of water on each side.

The Egyptians, all Pharaoh's horses, chariots and horsemen, pursued them into the sea. The Lord looked down and shot a pillar of fire and clouds at the Egyptian army, confusing the soldiers and frightening the horses. Then He made the wheels of their chariots come off.

Seeing this, the Egyptians said, "Let's get away from the Israelites! The Lord is fighting for them against Egypt."

Then the Lord said to Moses, *"Stretch out your hand over the sea so that the waters may flow back over the Egyptians and their chariots and horsemen."* Moses stretched out his hand and at daybreak the sea went back to its place. The Egyptians fleeing toward it were swept into the sea by the Lord." (Exodus 14-22-27)

The wall of the sea collapsed on both sides beginning at the base and until the two bodies of water met with a thunderous noise that shook the ground. The Ethiopian soldiers again fell to the ground as the impact and the force of wet air pushed the tide against the shoreline. Majestically, Moses turned and walked away without even a glance.

Silence followed and for hours no one moved. They slept wherever they lay, while the sea seemed to digest its victims. Most of the Israelites had not witnessed the closing of the sea and defeat of the Egyptian army because they were too far ahead.

Mericah whispered, "This is truly the God of gods. Such power is unthinkable; I will never question the God of Moses again. May he forgive me for worshiping the stone and gold faces of the gods of myth."

Then, for the first time in her life Mericah prayed to the spiritual God.

So many times she had unwillingly worshiped the stone faces of Egypt, the gold statues of the pharaoh, the sun, the wind, the stars of the night, the insignia's of prophets; even the dead kings of Raamsee. Now her mind was clear, her urge to say, thank you, I'm sorry, please and show me the way was overwhelming.

Among hundreds of her own people and the thousands of Israelites, with the bodies of Egyptian soldiers still being devoured by the Red Sea. While fear and amazement was so real and emotions seemed to be thickening the very air that we breathe, Mericah stood up. Those now standing around her involuntarily fell to their knees. A wave of people suddenly paused and stood motionless. Moses, Miriam and Aaron heard her voice as the very ears of God had opened to her. She slowly bowed her head and prayed as she had never prayed before.

"God ... All Mighty God ... We have seen and felt your presence. Our hearts hang heavy for we have ignored your expectations and we are proven incapable. We are unworthy of your care and yet you have not abandoned even the worst of us. Even the dead are at peace, for they have died by the hand of God. Yet...we stand on the shores of the Red Sea ... alive ... alive and helpless before you. Lead us as you may, to the purpose of our being. Forgive our daily resistance.

"Our fear of not knowing has caused our courage to hide. Our hearts are willing but weakness will not allow us to act in your way. As we journey blindly to you stumbling along the way, clear our paths oh . God, that the journey will not be so painful. All things grow toward you, we fall and we rise up and we rise up again and again and we will keep rising up until we are again cured of our sickness of ignorance. Until you, oh God can look upon your finished work with pride.

And you might say these are my own creation of which I am pleased. Like children, we will often do the wrong thing, go the wrong way, admire or even worship unbelievable fantasies. As a child looks to its mother for direction and understanding, we stand before you. I beg of you, Oh Mighty God, do as you will for the reasons only you could know, but bless us as your children with direction, understanding and unending forgiveness."

As her prayer ended there was stillness in the air, the sea had finally stopped churning. The mist of water seemed to vacuum its self away. The people began to move again as if released by a paralyzing hand, all seemed well; but Mericah knew the journey had just begun.

Chapter 6

The tribes of Israel had entered into the second month since leaving Egypt. The Ethiopians still remained at the rear of the masses. Some order had been established as the Lord God Almighty provided food and water. The anticipation of the land of milk and honey was on the mind of Mericah, though her heart still craved for the green homelands of her birthplace.

Samo, an Ethiopian captive who had lived in the chamber of virgins with Mericah had dedicated herself to serve the young princess; for she had eyes for Mohab the brother of Mericah and wished to become his first wife. The warm desert nights and the spectacle of the Exodus had brought Samo and Mericah closer together. The friendship presented a time for Samo to inquire about Mohab and the ways of their family.

"How old were you when you were taken from the homeland?" she asked Mericah.

"I'm not sure," she replied. "I believe, I may have been eight or nine years of age."

"Do you remember home?" Samo asked.

"I remember the celebrations of the hunts, the dancing before feast. The colorful wardrobes worn by the actors and especially the feast of fruits and juices of the tree nuts," answered Mericah.

As Samo and Mericah continued to talk, Mohab approached and was asked by Mericah why the Ethiopians permitted so many of their people to be taken by the Pharaoh's soldiers and why they had given the likes of Mericah without a declaration of war.

Mohab came close enough to be heard without raising his voice. As he began to tell the story of the Cushite Nation others gathered and came closer to hear for they, too, wondered why the powerful and proud Ethiopian warriors submitted to the Egyptians.

"It is recorded that many years ago Egyptians from the north and nomad groups from east of the Sinai came often to our great city of Napata. With them they brought hard metal products, fine pottery and never before seen; long knives and spears that were razor sharp to be used to hunt for wild game of the forest.

"Our people traded the yellow rocks of the sand beds that the Egyptians molded into gold objects of worship. The trading made many of the tribesmen of Ethiopia very strong and rich, in the eyes of the people of Ethiopia; throughout the land of Cush, Sudan and south beyond the southern dry lands.

"As the Egyptian items of trade became plentiful people found no reason to hunt stones for trade. There was no reason to constantly reap the harvest of our fruits, nuts and spices, for the Egyptians who had nothing else to trade.

"The Egyptians were given permission to search for precious stones and jewels in exchange for passage into the great city of Egypt,

The masters of Egypt possessed the gods. They possessed the temple that brought prosperity to kings of Cush. The pharaohs of Egypt began to deny access to the gods. The sicknesses of the northerners began to spread in our land and without access to the gods, Ethiopian people of royalty were exposed to the Egyptian illnesses and were dying.

"For the priest of the Pharaoh had convinced the kings of Ethiopia that neither everlasting life nor life after death could be achieved without the gods of Egypt. The aging and now frightened kings of the tribes of Cush wanted to live in the kingdom of heaven as they lived in the bountiful land of Ethiopia. They began to see the deaths of more and more of their countrymen. They made a pact to provide whatever Egypt wanted if they would ask the gods to stop the deaths and provide a place of life after death for their Ethiopian kings and royalty.

"The Pharaoh, in exchange for more gold and other imports, permitted our kings to send slaves to build temples as well as sending tributes to the gods, so they, too, could give praise and worship and reach eternity.

"As years passed, the people yearned for the simple days of godlessness, without the intimidation of the Egyptian soldiers. They began to resent being slaves and again shut down trade and access to our land for the Egyptians.

"The Pharaoh became angry with the Ethiopians and when a promise of more godly blessings failed the Pharaoh sent into Ethiopia the well-trained and merciless armies of Egypt to conquer and plunder all of Ethiopia and the land of Cush.

"'Bring back all of the gold and valuables that they possess!' the Pharaoh instructed. 'You may do as you please, but bring the young virgins back for the Pharaoh, bring back the young men to serve as slaves. Slay the elders and all the children, so they will not seek vengeance, as they become men. Also, bring me their king.'

"The land of Cush was divided into many tribes and had no unified forces to resist the Egyptians, for we had been a peace loving people whose needs were few. Within a year the whole occupied nation of Cush was plundered and free for all to ravage. Our father's father (a young man at the time) brought the remaining tribes together and retreated into the southern deserts to build, for the first time, a unified Ethiopian army. He vowed, he would avenge the deaths of his countrymen and kill even the gods of the Egyptians.

"While exiled, he received word that our father and his family had been captured by the Egyptian soldiers and was held captive in Nubia. With 5,000 foot soldiers, he intercepted and defeated the Egyptians. Our father and 1000 young men were rescued.

"The leading forces of the Egyptians had eluded the attack and made off with the captured young women including our princess, my sister, Mericah. For years, we have been building what is now a powerful army of more then 200,000 trained military men to drive the Egyptians into the sea. I have had no word from our land but by now I'm sure they have taken advantage of Egypt's weakness making the Pharaoh's army, no more.

"We must part from the Israelites as soon as the God of Abraham permits us and join our nation and God in the destruction of Egypt," Mohab proclaimed.

Chapter 7

Mericah had learned to pray to the God of Abraham, but had yet to hear from God or speak directly to Moses, as she had expressed. "Take me to Moses," she said to Mohab.

Mohab replied, "Moses has gone to the mount of Sinai for instructions from God and no one has seen him since. The Israelites are yearning to return to Egypt and have begun to worship a metal god Moses's brother, Aaron, has forged for them. It would be dangerous for any of us to be among the Hebrews, for they are a stupid and forgetful people who cannot obey God for their own sake."

"Then take me to the mountain. I will speak to Moses and God at once," she said.

Mohab resisted Mericah's request, only to earn her scorn. "Moses has gone in the wrong direction. I must tell him, and I must pray to God for the deliverance of Egypt into the hands of my father, as he delivered the chariots into the Red Sea. Take me to him or I will go without you, my brother."

Mohab led Mericah, first to the edge of the Israelites encampment and then to the foot of Mount Sinai. A glowing light rested upon the mountaintop above. As they approached the upward slope, the ground began to tremble. There was a low rumble like the deep tone of a running herd of elephants.

Suddenly, a man dressed in white clothing appeared out of the darkness. Slowly, he approached Mericah and Mohab. He appeared to be hundreds of years old. He was small in stature, with hair braided in an Ethiopian style.

"What is it that you want, Mericah?" he asked using the language of the people of Cush.

"Who are you?" she asked. "How do you know my name? Are you the God of Abraham?"

"I am just a voice," he said.

"I must speak with God!" she demanded.

"There is no need to speak with God. He knows of your request and it is already approved," he said in a tender and humble voice. "God has heard your mind and recognizes your heart of purity. The likes of you He has not found among the Israelites. Why are you not afraid of God, as your brother is?" the voice asked.

"I have done God no harm, I only wish to serve Him, as my brother, I am sure, wishes to defend Him with his life," she said.

"For your sake, your people will rise, fall and rise again in another land. For you shall have the blood of Moses, who is God's humble and chosen servant, running through the veins of your descendant."

"Who are you?" she asked again. "Are you an angel of God?"

He answered as he disappeared into the darkness. "I am just a voice. Your brother must leave, for Moses approaches with the glow of God upon his face. If he looks upon Moses, he will surely die."

Mohab bowed and backed away into the night to await his sister. As Mericah turned away from her brother and backed toward the voice, she found herself alone but unafraid.

Hours passed as she sat waiting for Moses. She fell into a deep sleep and dreamed that Moses instructed her to take his twin sons and the Ethiopians from a place called Kadesh and north to the Mediterranean sea. He said, "This is where your army will build ships to enter into a new promised land.

"Why have you come here?" Moses asked.

Mericah found herself wanting to kneel at his feet as she realized this was the man, who less than three months ago, forced the Pharaoh to free his people. Not by the force of an army, but by the demand of his God. This was the man who raised his hands and divided the sea. Now he stood before her puzzled by her presence and attracted to her courage as well as her beauty.

"Speak to me!" Moses said to her.

"I'm sorry," she said. "It's just that your face seems to be glowing. Your eyes are gentle yet there is anger there as well. I am not sure I am worthy to stand in your presence."

"Speak to me young woman. What is it that you want?" he asked.

"I have come to ask why you have chosen the desert land rather than the land of my people where you would be welcome and safe."

"Woman," he gently said, "it is not I who has chosen the path to the Promised Land. It was the choice of the Lord, thy God. When the spirit of God has possessed my mind and heart. I have no decisions to make." As he finished speaking he weakened and leaned against a stone for support.

"Leave my presence, for I am tired and in need of sleep. Tomorrow, I must deliver the word of God to my people, who have again tried the patience of the Lord."

Moses slowly slid down the stone and onto the ground. The fatigue had gotten the best of him, and he curled his body like a child and began to drift off to sleep.

Mericah turned and headed down the mountain. She heard a low moan from Moses as he turned over, trying to find comfort for his exhausted body. She called for Mohab who was not far away. "Bring my night pack and linens and return for me at the break of day. I have not completed my meeting with Moses."

Without question Mohab did what was asked and headed back to the campsite of the Ethiopians.

Mericah knelt at Moses' feet and loosened his sandals. She gathered underbrush and leaves from nearby bushes and put them next to him where he lay. She then located a trickling stream of water and moistened a linen cloth.

She gently removed his head garment and upper robe and washed his face and body as he lay sleeping. She took oils and cinnamon from her night sack and anointed his feet and legs, and the glow of his skin began recede. She then pulled his body onto the makeshift bedding.

When that was done, she stood motionless, gazing at the man called Moses as he lay there in the moon lit night. He was depleted of all his strength, yet still trying to live up to the wants and desires of his God even as he slept.

What a marvelous man; his God has chosen well, she thought. She sat down with him, then lifted his head and placed it onto her lap. While gently stroking his brows, she softly spoke to him, "Moses, where have you placed your heart? Is your love for the Israelites or for God? Who will reward this man called Moses for his unending sacrifice? Take me, oh Moses, take me with you that I, too, may win favor in the eyes of God. I too want to be worthy to enter into paradise on earth and in heaven. Maybe I can do it with this man so gentle, so strong."

She leaned toward him and laid her head upon his chest. Moses stirred slightly without waking, then they both fell into a deep sleep at God's very feet.

At the break of day they awoke lying face to face covered with only the linens Mericah had brought. Moses lifted himself up, covered Mericah, and then got up to get dressed so he could prepare to approach his people. He looked briefly at Mericah, reached out and touched her forehead, then turned and left.

As Mericah awoke, she wondered what had happened.

Suddenly an angel of God was standing near he. "Mericah," she said, "dress yourself and return to your people. Because of your fair and precious heart, you are now with child. Blessed is this child of Moses.

God will one day call His children, and your children's children will answer and receive their blessing. God will not forget you."

"Wait!" Mericah said while adjusting her clothing in a hurried fashion. "What is your name?"

"I am a voice and spirit. I am known not by title but by my presence," the angel responded.

"Where do you live?" Mericah asked.

The angel seemed uneasy with the question; knowing that there are some things that should not be known to man. Yet, she answered, "I live in the body of God the creator of man, in a place you might call heaven. A place of memory, a place where the spirit of God dwells, a place where righteousness comes naturally.

"What will become of my people?" Mericah asked.

The angel was trying to walk away from Mericah, but she followed and asked again. "What must my people do to receive God's favor?"

"The cry of your people pleases God, for he, too, feels the pain of his worldly creation. He will never be far from them. Though their cries will at times fall short of his ears. Your people of warm hearts will one day enjoy dwelling with His sons in the place of memory," the angel said, again turning to leave.

"Wait!" Mericah shouted. "Don't leave me! What shall I tell my people? They will question how a virgin can be with child and they will tum on me as a liar."

"Fear not, no heart shall tum against you, for God has made it so. I will always be with you. I cannot leave you alone. For we share the same spirit of God."

"How will I know when you are near?" asked Mericah.

"Every time you pray from your soul, you will feel the spirit that we share. Every time you feel love for another. Every time you shed a single tear of emotion. Every time you smile at the joyful sight of your children. Every time you draw a breath of air in appreciation of God's earthly beauties. When you feel the pleasure of someone else's happiness. When a gentle song touches your heart. When touching words of kindness reach your soul, at the death of a love one or the birth of a friend; all these things are a part of God's presence in man."

"And when I feel jealous? When I feel hate? When the desire of strike out at someone as part of my fury? And what of when, I am lustful or have the urge to become drunk from fermented wine or what of when I explore the existence of other gods or when I wish to say and do foolish things?" asked Mericah.

"Foolish things are a choice of men who wish make fools of themselves," the angel answered.

"Hateful, jealous things are a mystery to all, both in heaven and on earth, for just as foolish things are for fools, feeling hate and vengeance will cause the soul to slowly die. Nonetheless, God will still recognize all the good that is still left in a man. When his time comes, He alone will prune the dead branches from that life."

Mericah stood with her hands at her sides, without a single question left to ask. The angel smiled and bowed to her as she backed out of Mericah's presence.

"Why have you bowed to me? I am but a black slave," Mericah asked as the angel disappeared from view.

A voice, answered, "You are God's jewel and in your descendants there will always be remnants of the Holy One. Blessed are those who recognize the remnants of the seed of God."

"Mericah," Mohab said, "I have been looking for you. Why are you talking to a stone?" he asked.

Her attention was drawn to her brother, who was suddenly standing before her. She was looking around, still trying to see the angel. "Did you see her?" she asked. "Did you hear her voice?"

"No" Mohab responded. "Why are you glowing so radiantly? You look like you have been waxed in gold."

Mericah did not respond. She walked higher up the rocky slope, as if her brother was not there.

"Mericah, we need you," he said. "You are to be our queen. Please come back, for fear of God, I am afraid to go higher."

Mericah stopped in her tracks as she finally realized her brother's plea. With her back toward him she appeared to release her hold on a hand he could not see. As her right hand dropped back to her side. she turned to face Mohab. Confused, she looked over her shoulder and then back at Mohab, finally saying, "Let us leave here, my brother. The journey before us is long and there will be no resting place."

Chapter 8

The Ethiopians in the rear sector now numbered more than 10,000 and gathered along with another 6,000 people of mixed races who had joined them along the way. All had placed their faith into the hands of the God of the Hebrews. With thousands upon thousands of people spread over Sinai, rumors of disgruntled Israelites finally reached Mericah.

"What is wrong with those people? God has delivered them from the clutches of the Egyptians. As we speak, they are being lead to the Promised Land, yet they still defy the Lord's request."

"Look to the horizon," Mohab said to Mericah. "The desert sands in the distance are no longer flat and uneventful. The horizon is dotted with moving shadows that are distorted by the heat of the sun. There is an army of foot soldiers coming." He pointed from his left to right. His eyes were slightly squinted and the muscles in his upper cheeks flexed. Wearing the look of a mighty warrior who has just swallowed his fear, he turned away from Mericah and faced two of his Ethiopian comrades.

"Mount your horses and ride to them. By nightfall, you should be close enough to count their numbers without being seen. We will take our people into the foothills of God's mountain. There is no place else to run.

"I believe, they are the Pharaoh's army and some of his eastern allies. When you return, come to the hills just to the left of that rocky mound. A sentry will be looking for you. May the gods be with you," he said, as they scurried to obey his command.

Mohab then turned and faced six of his commanders who had approached while he was directing the scouts. "They appear to be moving south, toward us, at an unusually fast pace. Yet there is no dust cloud, which may mean there are no horsemen or chariots. How long do you think it will take them to reach us?" he asked one of the commanders.

"The sun is not yet at its peak, so we have at least eleven hours until nightfall. Considering the weight of their armor, they will not reach us for at least two days. This day and tomorrow will be our last without battle," the commander answered.

Mohab asked another commander "What are the Israelites doing?"

"They are camped starting just over there," he said, pointing. "All the way to the eastern side of the foot hills of Mt. Sinai. The largest body being just at the foothills, where Moses will gather the core of the families when he returns from God's mountain.

"Our scouts have reported that the Israelites in the northeast sector of the tribes have been moving north along the shoreline. It seems that they are headed toward the Sea of Jordan. We have learned there is water south, east and west of us. The only way to leave this place by land is north; the way we came. With the Israelites crowded by the thousands northeast of us, as I have said, it seems we have no choice but to take to God's mountain. There, we will die at the hands of God, for we have been warned of such. Or, we can penetrate the oncoming army at a northeast point with the Israelites at our back and rely upon our horses for a faster retreat. Even then, we would find ourselves cut off from our homeland and delivered into the hands of the tribes of the Canaanites, who are friendly to the Egyptians. We are, it seems, trapped again by the Pharaoh's army."

Mohab pondered his options as he turned his attention back to Mericah. "We must move our people east of here, into the foothills of

God's mountain," he told Mericah. "You must stay well within the crowd of Israelites until we clear a way through Pharaoh's army. Then we will make our way behind them, heading westward to the Sea of Reeds. We will hide there by night, then head south and home to our father."

"We must rely on the God of Moses, for he will not let us to be crushed after all we have seen," Mericah responded. "Take me back to Moses; he will speak with God."

Mohab had grown tired of being lead by Moses, since it was always seemingly in the wrong direction. He knew that the God of Moses had no love for the Ethiopians, for they had fallen prey to the gods of Egypt. The Ethiopians wanted to go home. They were slaves to the Egyptians and more than likely would become slaves to the Israelites. They longed for the days when they were not captives of another nation, when they simply lived to hunt and live off of the land.

"Moses has not been heard from since he returned to God's mountain and we don't have time to search for him. Furthermore, there are no waters to separate us from Pharaoh's slaughtering armies this time," he said.

"I will go there myself and pray to the God of Moses," Mericah said.

"We don't have the time," Mohab repeated.

"Bring me an ass," she demanded, refusing to put her confidence anywhere but into the hands of her newly found God.

Chapter 9

The journey to the base of the mountain where she had last seen Moses took nearly three hours. She felt that she must talk to God himself to warn Him about the approaching army and to tell Him and Moses that they have gone the wrong way.

One hour into her trip Mericah came upon the female angel of God sitting near the pathway to the mountain. "Where are you going Mericah?" she asked.

"I must speak with God!" Mericah said.

"Speak!" said the angel.

"No, you don't understand. I must speak with God himself," she said.

"I told you before, God hears you. You and your people have been heard."

"But we are trapped and heading again toward a sea. I must hear why from God. Why do you torment me with solemn smiles and gestures, while my people, God's people, are in danger?" she asked the angel in a sincere and pleading voice.

The angel walked up to Mericah and stroked the forehead of the ass on which she sat. With a comforting smile she said, "Your destiny and the destiny of your people is clearly written in the book of days to come. You will surely survive this desert voyage. For your people, the hardships to come will cause a yearning for God like no other children of God upon the face of the earth have experienced. You and your people have learned to look inside where God has planted seeds of compassion."

"Are you not listening to me at all?" Mericah asked. "There is no time for riddles. God shall surely punish you severely when He hears of your refusal to bring me into His presence. Move aside so I may proceed, for the breath of the Pharaoh's armies is upon my people and yours."

On her way again, Mericah rode as fast as she could toward God's mountain. After riding for close to an hour, she again came upon the same female angel of God waiting in the center of the path.

"What is it with you?" she asked in a frustrated voice. "How is it that you travel so fast and yet you waste time standing around? Move aside so I will not be forced to ride around you."

The ass she was riding slowed to a walk and then came to a complete stop as the angel again placed her hand on its forehead.

"I will pay you dearly to take me to God on your horse," Mericah said.

"I have no horse," replied the angel. 'I know you Mericah," she said while still looking directly at the ass. "I have seen you crying as you miss the caresses from your mother. I have heard your plea to be a mother. I have seen your dream to heal the pains of your people."

Mericah looked down at the angel, amazed, and asked, "Are you God or not? If not, how do you know these things and why are you still in my way?"

"God is with you Mericah," said the angel.

Mericah heard her brother's voice up ahead. "What has God said?" asked Mohab.

She realized she was back among her people. "I am confused," she said. "I must've gotten lost...or turned around. I have not seen God. Help me down."

Mohab held the ass with one hand and assisted Mericah with the other.

"We are not moving fast enough." Mohab said. There are so many of us and we are inspired to leave no one behind, so it is slow going."

"You say you are moving slowly and yet you've caught up with me." Before she ended her sentence there was a sudden stillness, then total silence followed by the voice that all could hear.

All of the Ethiopians and all of the Israelites who were spread for miles at the foot of Mt. Sinai heard the following:

"I am the Lord your God, who brought you out of Egypt, out of the wind of slavery. You shall have no other gods before me. You shall not make for yourself an idol in the form of anything in heaven above or on the earth beneath or in the waters below.

"You shall not bow down to them or worship them, for I the Lord your God am a jealous God, punishing the children for the sin of the fathers to the third and forth generation of those who hate me; but showing love to a thousand generations of those who love me and keep my commandments.

"You shall not misuse the name of the Lord your God for the Lord will not hold anyone guiltless who misuses his name.

"Remember the Sabbath day by keeping it holy. Six days you shall labor and do all your work, but the seventh day is a Sabbath to the Lord your God. On it you shall not do any work, neither you nor your son or daughter, nor servants, nor your animals, nor the alien within your gates.

For in six days the Lord made the heavens and the earth, the sea and all that is in them,' but he rested on the seventh day. Therefore, the Lord blesses the Sabbath day and made it holy."

"Honor your father and your mother, so that you may live long in the land the Lord your God is giving you.

"You shall not murder. You shall not steal. You shall not give false testimony against your neighbor. You shall not covet your neighbor's wife or his servants or anything that belongs to another."

The people saw the thunder and the lightning, heard trumpet and saw the mountain in smoke, and they trembled with fear. (Exodus 20-18)

Chapter 10

The Ethiopians fell to the ground and would not look up at the mountain for fear that God would know they had already sinned against the Lord. Mericah had fallen to her knees and had been overcome by the spirit of God. An aura of God had surrounded her as her beautiful face again gazed upward into the heavens as she prayed.

"Forgive us, Oh Lord God Almighty, for we as a people have sinned against you. We are powerless against the foolishness of our whims. Our judgment is lacking without your presence as the ruthless armies are nearly upon us. Let us join the people of God that we to may have the opportunity to learn your ways and serve but one God."

She stood upright and listened for a response from God. But instead there was a low-pitched humming sound coming from the desert. Thousands of soldiers had now overtaken the people of the exodus. The humming grew louder as the soldiers quickly approached. The humming sounded like a song with a rhythm that matched the footsteps of the oncoming soldiers; a song that set the cadence of attack with the beating of spears against animal skin shields.

The Ethiopian soldiers realized that the voice of God had stopped and the sound of thousands of warriors had taken the place of God's voice. The Ethiopians got up immediately and ran for their own swords and shields. For death was surely at their door. The humming suddenly stopped and the rumble of footsteps also came to a halt as thousands of oncoming soldiers stomped against the ground with a few more steps and then stood motionless and without a sound.

Mericah looked at the crowd of soldiers who were lined a hundred deep and from left to right as far as she could see,

"The Lord has seen fit to end our lives at the hands of our enemies," she thought to herself. But she did not recognize the colors of the shields, for they were not like any she had seen in Egypt. The men, the soldiers faces were black .. .like her own ... they were all black...

Her brother, after realizing that the attacking army was an army of black men, shouted aloud, "They are Cushites! They are from our Ethiopian homeland! They are our people! God has spared us from sure death."

Mohab went forward toward the Ethiopian army, speaking the language of his homeland as many others also went to welcome the soldiers with the food and water God had provided from the heavens. Word spread rapidly through the soldiers of their homeland, that they had found the lost children of Hamron, ruler of Ethiopia.

Chapter 11

With more than forty thousand armed Ethiopian Cushite foot soldiers between Mericah and the Egyptian army, and hundreds of thousands of Israelites in pursuit of God's land of milk and honey, she had never felt so secure, though she hadn't yet told her brother that she was with child. As she lay in her tent with Mahlah, a Hebrew slave who had become close to her in Egypt, Mahlah asked who had fathered the child she was carrying.

"I am not sure," responded Mericah. "I can only slightly remember falling into a deep sleep while lying in the arms of Moses at God's mountain. I have not been near any other man and yet I am with child. I am uneasy about making an announcement about my condition to my brother and my people for fear that Mohab may want to take the life of Moses."

"Are you fond of Moses?" asked Mahlah.

"I think so. In a brief moment on God's mountain when we were alone, I sensed his gentleness and his need to be caressed. Yet, there is something in the way he looked into my soul that made me know he is doing God's work and he will not let his own desires stand in the way of his commitment to Israel. It's as if he spoke through his heart saying, I'm sorry; I am not permitted to love anyone but God. During those few hours together, I yearned for him as I have sometimes yearned to be with my family as a child. Beyond the yearning, I was overwhelmed with wanting to submit to him. Being in his presence weakened my resistance to being touched."

Mericah continued, "Now, I am carrying a child and I am no man's wife. After years of accepting I would always be a virgin and knowing that I would be buried alive with the body of the Pharaoh, where I would live forever with riches and servants at my feet in paradise, I find myself in this strange position. I am alive and surrounded by the constant threat of war and death, with a new God, in a place I have never heard of.

"I no longer want to die for the sake of life. Now I want to live for the sake of the life I carry in my womb. Now I want to live in the light of the God that made me a seeing and understanding woman. Yet, these changes have come so quickly. I'm afraid, but I don't know what I am afraid of." She paused and bowed her head as her shoulders slumped in sadness.

"I am told that I am special, yet I only want to be humble ... as humble as this man Moses, who I believe is somehow the father of my child." Mericah looked up at Mahlah as if seeking advice from her friend, then asked, "How, with all that is happening, do I tell my brother and my people I have been dishonored by an Israelite who believes in the living God of Abraham? What shall I say?"

"Don't worry," said Mahlah, "our God is a powerful, all knowing God. Pray to Him. I know He will make you strong. I will speak with Moses, he is a fair man, he will ask God to—"

"No!" Mericah interrupted. "You must not speak to Moses about me. His mission is not to serve a woman."

"Then I will speak to Miriam, his sister," said Mahlah. "She will know what to do."

When Mahlah told Miriam that an Ethiopian woman was carrying the child of Moses, she looked at Mahlah with fury in her eyes. "This cannot be, the woman is lying! Take me to he right this moment," she demanded

"Why are you so angry? She has been touched by the God of Abraham and she, too, wishes to serve God and worship His name."

"No!" Miriam snapped back. "She is not like us, we are Hebrew, she is Egyptian. There is no difference between Egyptian and Ethiopia, they are all Cushite."

"But she has been freed from bondage just as we have," said Mahlah, "She, too, left the Pharaoh and the harsh hand of the Egyptians. She is royalty in her homeland and a strong, worthy woman; worthy of bearing strong children and teaching the ways of Abraham. Please don't curse her for not being born to a Hebrew," Mahlah pleaded.

"Take me to her, she and her people must leave us," said Miriam. Miriam's heart was hardened toward Mericah, and she would not listen to reason.

As she entered the camp of the Ethiopians, she became even more angry than before. She didn't know there were so many Cushites mingling with the Hebrew descendants of Dinah, the thirteenth child of Jacob and only daughter of the son of Isaac.

"I am Miriam," she said. "I am the sister of Moses and Aaron. I am here to warn you that you and your tribe do not belong here. God has instructed Moses to bring us into a land chosen for the children of Israel. You must not be so bold as to stand against the will of the God of Israel. God will crush anyone who opposes his promise to Abraham."

"But we are not here to stand against God," Mericah said, "We are standing with you against the Pharaoh. We wish to worship your God as you do. Is God just for the Israelites? Does He belong only to Miriam?"

These questions angered Miriam even more, for Miriam had named herself a prophetess of God. She felt that if God had wanted these Egyptians or Ethiopians (they were the same to her) he would surely make it known to her or to Moses or Aaron. There was no such confirmation.

"If you do not take your people and leave, God will consume them into the earth and they will be no more," Miriam said.

"Let me speak to God, so that I may ask his blessing to let us leave peacefully and reach our homeland without the wrath of the Pharaoh," Mericah pleaded with Miriam.

"God is with Moses," Miriam said, "He will be with Moses until we enter the Promised Land. Let your god lead you, he is the god that has come against us for the last time. Let him take you and your people home," responded Miriam. With that she walked away, turning her back to Mericah and those who were present, including Mohab.

"She has spoken the truth, my sister," Mohab said. "We should be leaving this desert land and going back to the land we have reclaimed."

Mericah felt faint and weak with confusion. She could not disagree with her brother, although she wanted desperately to speak with Moses. She instructed Mohab, "Lead our people home."

Chapter 12

Two weeks after leaving the Israelites, Ethiopian scouts spotted a brigade of Egyptian soldiers northeast of the sea of reeds. They seemed to be waiting for the Ethiopians to fall back into their arms as slaves; for there was no other way, by land, to reach Cush, other than through Egypt. The Egyptian army was still too strong for the Ethiopians in a direct battle. The Ethiopian army now numbered more than sixty thousand with less than two thousand horsemen. Their strength was their trained foot soldiers. The foot soldiers could run a foot for ten miles to fight without resting and were a viable match for the Egyptian swordsmen. The Ethiopian army was much stronger with the distant spears.

Mohab called his officers to his side. Instinctively, he instructed one officer to take eight hundred men and place themselves east of the Egyptian army towards southern Canaan. He instructed them to place themselves far enough to barely be seen. At daybreak, they were to draw the attention of the Egyptians and pretend to flee eastward as fast as they could run. He instructed another group to go into the Egyptian camp and inform them that this small group of eight hundred, are Hebrew and that Moses is among them and that further east are the virgin captives and the gold of the Ethiopians that were taken during the exodus.

Mohab placed his two thousand horsemen out of sight just south of the Egyptians.

One of the officers questioned, "Why are we not attacking during the night and slaughter them while they sleep?"

"We are not cowards who stumble in the dark among thousands of trained Egyptian soldiers to our own sure death. Those are the tactics of Canaans when they out number their enemy by thousands. We want them to know who they have come against," Mohab said. Finally, he lined twenty thousand of his fastest armed foot soldiers at the rear of his horsemen.

When morning came, the Egyptians could faintly see at a distance, the fleeing soldiers who they thought were Hebrews with Moses among them, running towards the safety of the masses of Israelite tribes rumored to be further east. With two thousand chariots and another ten thousand horsemen, the Egyptians charged in full speed to slaughter the, thought to be, helpless Hebrews. The remaining heavily armored Egyptian foot soldiers were running behind all of them, anxious to make a kill. It was nearly mid-day when the chariots and horsemen over took the eight hundred disguised Ethiopian fighting men, who were fighting bravely but were no match for the twelve thousand mounted soldiers.

The sound of battle ahead caused the Egyptian foot soldiers to scatter while running nearly a quarter of the day to participate in the slaughter. They ran and ran yelling with mayhem in their hearts. They could smell the blood of the enemy, as they became more and more reckless in their attack.

Mohab gave the signal for his horsemen to attack from behind. In full stride the Ethiopian horsemen over ran the running foot soldiers. In silence they wiped out hundreds of straggling soldiers and then into the center of the charging Egyptians, killing thousands with the Egyptians still unknowing that they are being over run from the rear. The Ethiopian foot soldiers were given the signal to pick up the slain Egyptian's shields and helmets and to continue the attack from the rear of the Egyptians. The Ethiopian horsemen were signaled to pull out of the pursuit and regroup behind their own foot soldiers, now dressed and disguised as Egyptian soldiers.

After hours of battle, the Egyptian horsemen and remaining chariots were far ahead and out of the sight of their own foot soldiers. After the slaughter of the eight hundred Ethiopian decoys, they were still in full stride trying to catch up to the non-existing Hebrews who were thought to be headed for Canaan. By nightfall, thousands of Egyptians lay dead on the sands east of the sea. The Ethiopians lost less than fifteen hundred soldiers, as the entire Egyptian army of the foot soldiers were dead or captive.

The following morning the Egyptian horsemen and chariots had camped and were awaiting their foot soldiers for water and food before continuing their quest. When the disguised Ethiopian foot soldiers came into view of the Egyptian horsemen, Mohab signaled a group of soldiers he had placed through out the night, to appear to be attacking their own marching Ethiopian comrades with their backs to the Egyptian horsemen. The Egyptian horsemen and chariots mounted their attack on the rear of the Ethiopians while Mohab signaled his own horsemen, also dressed and disguised as Egyptian horsemen, to again come up the rear of the Egyptians.

Mohab had instructed his ground soldiers not to turn and face the enemy until they were within the striking distance of the Ethiopian spears. When the Egyptians finally began to engage some of the Ethiopians, the Ethiopian horsemen had already began their assault at the rear of the charging Egyptians, again without being noticed. When the Ethiopians were given the signal to lodge their spears all at once, thousands of spears were air borne and raining onto the oncoming, unsuspecting Egyptian horsemen. By early evening the battle had ended.

"Gather the captives and the Egyptian horses," Mohab said as he sent word through out his men that they were excellent in battle and they would be rewarded, not only with spoils of the battle, but status and property when they reached their homeland.

That night, the Ethiopians celebrated their victory with music and dance as the leading officers met to plan the next steps to reaching their homeland. Most of the captives of the battle gladly abandoned the Pharaoh in exchange for their lives and swore to support the Ethiopians, others were sent eastward into the, not so friendly, hands of the Canaanites.

"I find no pleasure in the taking of so many lives," said Mohab to his officers.

"The Egyptian army has forced many of us into war for the sake of our own survival. For the sake of their own god, they have shown no mercy to thousands of our tribesmen. Still, we will tend to their wounded as our own. We will take two days to prepare and bury our dead in this foreign land, then we will proceed on our quest to reach our home."

All of the officers agreed and disbanded to their perspective obligations. Mohab proceeded back to the campsite of the women and children. His arms were weary from the many blows he had struck in his first battle against the Pharaoh's armies. He was moved inwardly by the thought that so many had died in such a short period of time.

During the short journey towards camp, Mohab like Mericah, encountered a black female standing directly in his path.

"Greetings," he said while wondering what such a young and beautiful maiden was doing here alone in this no-man's land.

"Greetings, Mohab," she said while smiling kindly and slightly tilting her head to one side.

Mohab dismounted and approached her with his hand extended to greet her in friendship. "Do I know you?" he asked.

"I know you," she said. "I was there when you were lost near the den of lions."

Mohab paused in disbelief, for he recalled that he was only nine years old when he had gotten lost and wandered into a lion's den. He had not realized the danger of being eaten alive. He remembered lying down and curling his small body in fear as the huge, beastly lions ran toward him, thinking he was their prey. In fear, he had lost consciousness.

He was afraid that he would be devoured. The roar of two lions awakened him. Both were above him, circling. Every time the other lions came near, the two large male lions would roar and claw at them viscously. Feeling exhausted and safe between the lions, he went back to sleep. When he opened his eyes again at daybreak, he heard his father's voice.

"Son? Son, where are you?" his frantic father shouted at the top of his lungs.

"Here, Father. I am here," he recalled answering as he ran toward his father, who had just come into view.

"Where are the lions?" he asked his father.

"There are no lions son."

"But, Father, they were here. They were all around and they roared and fought all through the night," he remembered saying.

"Thank the gods, son, that you were only dreaming," his father said.

"But Father, they were here," he said, pointing at all of the disturbed and broken shrubbery. "See the blood on the ground and rocks."

As a nine year old telling a story no one believed, he had carried that experience through the years, and it was known only to him.

"I would not let them harm you then and I will not let the Pharaoh harm you now," the angel said.

Mohab immediately fell at her feet. "You are the goddess," he said aloud. "What shall I do for you? I'm sorry," he said, though he wasn't sure of what he was sorry for.

"You are forgiven," said the angel. She gently pulled him to his feet. He stood towering over her by more than a foot. She looked up into his eyes as might a mother, yet she appeared to be his age or younger.

"I'm not a goddess, I am one of many voices," she said. "The Lord God Almighty has spoken through me for many years. You must listen to me, for what I am about to say is the way of God. Gather the bodies of the Egyptians your people have slain. Prepare their bodies as they do in their own land. Wrap them in linen, which will be provided for you, and entomb their corpses, for though they are blind, God has not lost love for them. Their place, too, has been prepared according to their beliefs. Do not leave even one body to the vultures or to rot in the sun. When the burial is complete, go on your way, remain pure at heart and you and your people will be blessed."

Mohab stood patiently waiting for the angel to complete her instructions. "I have not been on the side of your God and I don't know His name or how to worship Him," he said.

"I know you have not been on His side but He has always been on yours. To love your people has been God's pleasure. They have been known to cause hurt to themselves, yet their faith is and always will be unwavering. Your burdens will cause many to give thanks to God that they are not of a dark race and yet many will question why they cannot attain your stamina and endurance. You will one day be embraced in the bosom of God."

Mohab began to speak, but she had disappeared from view, so he was left awkwardly talking to himself. Mohab looked every which way but she had gone. "There was no one there but me," he said, while mounting his horse.

"Just me and the lions," he mumbled, "Just me and the lions."

Chapter 13

Mericah, the women and children, who were left in the safety of the camp, had received word of victory over the massive army of the Pharaoh. The people were filled with joy, but Mericah remained uneasy about the still unforeseen destiny of her people.

Mohab entered the tent of Mericah. H e was more exited about his experience with the angel than the victory in battle.

"Why are you bursting with such pride my brother," she asked in jest.

"It was true, it was not a dream," he said boasting.

"What are you talking about?" she asked.

"She was there, she… he paused after realizing he could never explain his encounter. "Never mind," he said. "I have decided to take the time to bury the Egyptian dead."

His decision to remain on the battle scene puzzled Mericah. After he explained what the black angel said, she understood and gave her support to her brother's decision.

Reluctantly, she used this occasion to inform her brother of her childbearing condition. "I am with child," she whispered.

"What?" he asked.

"I am with child," she repeated.

Mohab looked like a child himself, shaking his head no, as if to say, you are in trouble. "But how can you be with child my sister? What will we tell our people?"

"I will tell them it is the choice of the God of Israel, for I believe the child carries the blood of Moses."

Mohab lifted his head a little higher. He took in a deep breath in an attempt to restrain his anger and impulse to chase down Moses and the Israelites and slay them, one after the other. "We will bury the dead first and then we will pursue them and take their dream away."

"No, you will not," said Mericah. "The God of Israel has made it so. Who are you to question what He has chosen to do?"

Mohab was still unable to control all of his anger against his beloved sister. "God has not given you a child. Moses has dishonored our family and our nation, for you are not his wife or his concubine. No one can violate the princess of all of Cush and live. I personally must take his life or you must die in his place."

Mericah had not realized the implications of her pregnancy. According to customs, the child of Moses would have the supreme right to rule Cush and most of the people of Upper Egypt. It meant that the Hebrew child would become a king of the nation of Cush and its newly trained army, which was prepared to defeat the Pharaoh and win back their rites, according to the laws of war.

The Cushites intentions were to defeat the Pharaoh's army, capture or kill Ramsee and return to power with Mericah as their queen. Her children would reign, and were supposed to be Ethiopian children, not Egyptian, not northern Nubians and surely not an Israelites.

"Please do not take my life nor the life of Moses, for he has meant no harm to us. I swear to you, it was God's will and if not God, it was surely my own weakness. I, alone, was tempted. I, alone, could not resist the thought of being caressed by the man of God. It was I who put myself against his body. I'm only human my brother... I am so sorry now, but I cannot change what is done. Please help me. I have prayed to the God of Israel, the gods of Egypt and the god of Cush. They have all turned their backs on me in the disgusted way of man. The gods have turned against me, will you also? You would take the life of your father's daughter, the princess who you have risked your life to protect?"

"You do not have love for this man called Moses. He has tricked you into submission and now he wishes to take his people into Cush, where his child will rule. Upon his death, the child will be a Cushite. I'm sorry my sister, he must die. Tell no one of this. I will speak with my brothers, we will decide who the father is."

Mohab began to make his exit when Mericah spoke again. "I think I love him," she whispered. Then she loudly asked, "Would Egyptian blood in my child's veins be acceptable to our god and not the blood of a Hebrew. We have seen the power of the Hebrew God. Is He to be denied as the Supreme God by you? Most of the Hebrews are black like me. Are they not truly the descendants of the Cushites? Surely he must not be put to death."

"Still, the laws of our land must not be compromised. There has been no marriage, and our father has been dishonored. The pride of Ethiopia would be a laughing matter to all of Cush that we, too, are like those from the north who mate and bare children at random. The laws pertaining to virgins are honored even in Egypt. Why should Moses be excluded?" Mohab asked, and left her tent to call his leaders and troops to a meeting.

"First we shall entomb the dead Egyptian soldiers. Then we shall march on the Israelites." The Ethiopian commanders were taken aback by this new command, but said nothing. Mohab's aura of authority had changed; he was now a man filled with vengeance and obviously someone to be reckoned with.

Mericah decided that she must warn Moses. She thought an attack on Moses and God would mean the death of her own people without mercy, just like the deaths of the Egyptian soldiers at the Red Sea. She began again to pray to the God of Israel. She prayed again and again, but there was no answer, no voice, nothing ...

When that didn't work, she had someone bring her a small golden god of Egypt. She then prayed to the god as she had so many times before.

"Why are you speaking to a stone, Mericah?" a voice echoed in her head, "Are you a fool or the fool of fools?" Immediately Mericah stood up and knocked the golden god to the ground as if it were to blame for her foolishness. She wiped her hands frantically as if trying to remove honey from her fingers.

"You cannot wipe your heart or your soul of guilt, just as you cannot wipe away your hope that someone will listen to just you, when you choose to be heard."

Mericah, inspired by her own raw courage, lifted her head in anger and said, "Then why are you tormenting me? Why don't you give us peace of mind? Why must there be turmoil and crisis after crisis, and men filled with ego and customs without end? You have made us fools and now we run from place to place to seek a place of worship, only to find that the god has changed or another god has replaced the last. One day they are man, then they are stone, the sun, the water, the mountain and now just a voice. What are we to be other than fools if we are being made fools of by the games of gods."

"The choice has always been yours," said the voice.

"No," Mericah interrupted, "The choice has never been ours. We are but sheep being led in circles and punished for going the wrong way. Tug the rope and I am pulled this way and that; loosen the rope and I lay down. 'Oh no, you say, you should not have lain down, you have offended the gods.' I am tired of all gods," she said with the tears streaming down her cheeks and also inwardly falling onto her heart where they burned like acid.

The voice was again silenced by Mericah's attack. There was an extremely long silence and then a softer, milder voice of another. "I am," he said and paused, "I am the voice to the wise and to the foolish. God is not in the presence of man to be given sacrifice or worship. He is and always will be a voice of help for mankind. God has no need for what men have to offer. God does not seek to confuse man. He seeks only to direct mankind toward the many paths that may lead him to his own happiness during the stages of earthliness.

"Many gods have failed because they exist only in the minds of men; yet, they have grown to be powerful protectors of the living and absolute saviors of the dead, from now and into eternity. Some of mankind has chosen to exalt themselves to the level of God and have brought their many gods along to glorify their personal images. God does not seek to credit Himself with the achievements of man; for the achievements of men are measured by the astonishments of their own peers and how well they serve their own needs. Every living being in heaven and on earth, with the ability to reason, must set its own boundaries of belief; be it way of life, worship or death.

"Moses has been chosen to record and deliver to his people a history and a way of life that relates to the expectations of the descendants of Abraham and to present laws necessary for mankind to evolve. Just as you chose to pray before a golden stone, many before you, who have been chosen for God's reasons have gone outside the boundaries of sensibility, beyond even the expectations of the Almighty. They have created all manners of gods, both good and evil. Many have deceived the innocent and walked among men as gods themselves. They are lofty and self-adorned with arrogance and pride.

"Because of man's natural desire to find and love his creator, they are willing to subject themselves to the follies of self-appointed messengers — messengers who have projected themselves as prophets and interpreters of dreams. These god-like messengers have found pleasures in being praised and bowed down to. They have convinced the children of God that praise and burnt offerings are needs of the Almighty.

"In truth, God accepts the praises and such, for the sake of man's self-acknowledgment and man's self-desire to be closer to God. Do not kindle your anger against God because you cannot understand the continuing creation of mankind. Only God knows the destiny of billions upon billions of souls. Accept that the blood of God runs through your veins. All will not go your way. All will not go the way of God.

"Be advised, when you or your people choose to stray from God's way, which is written in your heart and will be written as the word of

God, you will suffer long; not by the hand of God but by the hands of the gods men have created for themselves.

"Don't be shamed by the conception of a child of Moses, he is chosen by God. All who harm you or the descendants of your children will loose their place when they answer to God's servants."

Mericah was entranced by the voice and began to stir as silence returned. "May I speak to you again?" she asked.

"Yes," answered the gentle voice.

"Bless my people that they, too, may enjoy the spirit of God for years to come, and that we may live in the presence of God for eternity," said Mericah.

"God has blessed all of mankind. Do not be deceived by hardships and defeat as you stand before man. God will open all eyes in due time and you shall stand before Him and recognize the strength of your soul. Remember one step does not complete a journey," with this final word the voice again was silent.

Mericah became submissive, for she had satisfied her fears with the spirit of God. She breathed deeply and slowly as awareness of her environment began to return. She pondered her encounter with the voice, which she assumed belonged to an angel of God. The mere presence of the Holy Spirit enhanced her understanding far beyond her own years.

She asked herself, "What did the voice mean when he said, 'one step does not complete a journey'? Does it mean that life as we know it is just a part of our growth toward eternal life or does it mean that we shall die more than once before being eternally dead?

"Did he not say that God has no need to be worshiped and that man has developed his many ways of prayer because of his own need to receive praise and expects the Almighty to desire as he does?

Where do I stand in the eyes of God? she wondered. *Why have I been chosen to bear the child of the Israelite called Moses? Why do I yearn more and more to be in the presence of Moses, even more than I yearn for my newly found God?*

Chapter 14

Mohab buried thousands of slain Egyptians, as the angel had instructed him to do. During the burial effort, Mohab had sent out six horsemen to scout for the Israelites.

They had returned to report their observations to their leader. "The Israelites have massed by the thousands, just south of a place called Kamish. Moses has set up a tent northeast of the main encampment. They have not been moving from to place for weeks. The people are awaiting further instructions from Moses," reported one of the scouts.

Mohab gathered his most elite soldiers and instructed them to head north of the Israelites, in the direction they had been moving before stopping to camp. His plan was to stop the movement of the masses by threatening an attack and hopefully drawing Moses away from the soldiers of Joshua. Mohab had no quarrel with the Israelites, but he felt that Moses had broken the law of the land by violating his sister without marriage. He felt that the gods would recognize his rights, by the law, to take the life of the violator. If the Israelites chose not to honor the law and defend Moses, his soldiers would be positioned to extract Moses while Mohab's soldiers retreated without battle.

Once Mohab had set the stage, he took thirty men and made his way among the Israelites to locate and take the life of Moses. Mohab and the thirty soldiers made their way presumably towards their target. Before the Ethiopians found Moses, he and Aaron approached and confronted the Ethiopians!

Moses walked directly up to Mohab, who had drawn his sword, as his soldiers circled Moses and cut off any possible retreat. Moses fearlessly stood face to face with Mohab and asked, "Why have you come to do me harm?"

Mohab had drawn his arm back in preparation for a forward thrust of sure death for Moses, but his ability to strike was strangely impaired.

"Wait," Moses said, "Why are you filled with anger against me? I have done nothing, nor will I do anything to harm you or your people."

Still angered and yet unable to strike, Mohab answered, "You have made a harlot of my sister and you shall not live to do the same to other young maidens."

"Wait! I have not touched your sister. Tell me who you are and your sister is."

Mohab, stuttering, raised his arm across his chest from right to left as if to back hand Moses with his sword, only to find his downward thrust still blocked by some unseen force. He did not want to talk; he wanted to make the kill. He desperately wanted to avenge his sister. "She was so important to his homeland. She was to be the pride of her people, the queen of all the land from Egypt to southern Ethiopia; now, she is with child and unwed. Even the Pharaoh had the respect not to take her virginity. The people of Cush have been violated just as surely as she was." Again, he attempted to complete the strike to the neck of Moses and again he could only draw upward.

"Wait!" Moses repeated. "You are mistaken. I don't know your sister."

The commotion drew the attention of armed Israelites standing nearby. They began to gather and come to the aide of their leader. Mohab had waited too long. The element of surprise was gone. The chance to slay Moses and exit safely had passed. The Israelite men wrestled Mohab to the ground with very little resistance. The other thirty Ethiopians were outnumbered by hundreds of Israelites who had realized there was an attempt to harm Moses.

"Wait!" Moses exclaimed. "Don't harm him. Let him up." They lifted Mohab up, but continued to restrain his arms.

"Let him go," said Moses. "Tell me, who is your sister?"

"Mericah is my sister. The same Mericah I left to speak with you at God's mountain."

Moses' mouth fell open as his eyebrows lifted in surprise. He remembered her and said, "Come with me," as he began walking away toward his tent. "Leave us alone," Moses gestured with his arm." Reluctantly the Israelites began to loosen their grasp on Mohab.

"Let him go, I say," said Moses.

Moses and Mohab made their way into the tent where they were finally alone.

Moses, standing directly in front of Mohab, bowed his head and said, "As God is my witness, I cannot recall violating your sister ... and yet...I know the child is mine and I know she is my wife. God, Himself, has given her to me. There has been no transgression. Until now, I have been unaware of her. I thought she was a dream. She is my wife, this I know without a doubt."

"How can she be?" asked Mohab, skeptically. "There have been no vows or acceptance from any authority or holy minister." Mohab's anger was beginning to subside. Strangely, he began to reason that if the God of Moses had chosen Mericah, she must truly be destined to lead the Ethiopians to the one and only most powerful God. The Pharaoh and the gods of Egypt could not match His power. Maybe this was a heavenly marriage.

"Do you love my sister?" Mohab asked, "for she is special beyond even your imagination."

Moses raised his head and looked into Mohab's eyes. "I feel a love for all of God's children that I cannot describe with words. I have only laid eyes upon Mericah once and then, it was in the presence of God. I know now she is my wife, who I can no longer live without; yet, the Almighty God is in constant demand of my many other emotions. He has left me no space or time for an expression of love. She must love and receive love from our children for the God of our father has already made it so. My time now is for Gods purpose. Our bond has more reason than short term emotions or long term affections."

Mohab began to respect and admire the gentle strength Moses projected as he spoke. He could hear compassion in his voice that he had not heard in any man before. Mohab felt safe in the presence of Moses, safe from the feeling of caution and feelings of errors or fears of what god or man he should trust. He knew he could trust Moses and he knew Moses was on a mission. This mission had no place for the people of Cush at this time. Mericah was now the common ground between these two nations of people.

The two men talked long into the night as men; men who had both sacrificed their lives to live out the expectations of others — one a man of this God, and the other, his nation. They parted with an understanding that each were merely pawns; pawns by choice, but still merely pawns.

On this day they were headed in different directions but Moses assured Mohab that they would meet again where there would be no threat of wars. They would meet in a place where the Almighty would show His face to all.

Chapter 15

Mericah was desperately trying to reach Moses before her brother found him. She wanted to warn him. She wanted to tell him to ask his God for protection. She was fully aware of her brother's courage and his devotion to the customs of Ethiopia.

It was well into the night when she reached the tent of Moses. She made Moses aware of her arrival and received permission to enter his tent. She stood trance-like before him. She was delighted to find him alive. She was nervous and remained silent momentarily as she turned and twisted her fingers between each other like a bashful child.

Moses stood up and gazed at her. He, too, was mesmerized and found himself shyly staring back at her. Mericah took several steps toward him. She stopped and again displayed her child-like gestures. The light from a lantern struck her face and highlighted her slender black neck and beautiful body. Moses watched her step toward him and he walked closer to the beauty he had already claimed as his wife.

Mericah bowed her head in submission, while clenching her fists and moving her hands in a tense fashion. She bit her bottom lip and glanced upwardly for a split second. Her eyes were sparkling as if they had captured all the secrets of a starlit night.

Moses took a deep breath and extended his left hand, although she was still far beyond his reach. She could feel her knees buckle slightly as she yearned to rush into his arms. She looked up into his eyes again and walked slowly toward him. His other arm was now raised creating a wall of arms and robe leading directly to his chest — the chest of a humble man. A chest that contained a heart of gold. A chest that God Himself had favored to bear the responsibility of a nation.

Mericah could no longer stand. She suddenly collapsed just as Moses grabbed her. He pulled her into his arms and held her tightly, as if he hadn't seen her for years. Oddly, he wasn't even sure of her name. He stood inhaling the smell of her scented hair. He hugged her as tightly as he could without harming her.

She, in turn, buried herself in his embrace. She clung to his robe and closed her eyes as she silently wept. "Please, just hold me for a moment," she begged.

A few moments passed and Moses moved slightly, "No, not yet," she said. "Not yet, I cannot stand. My heart has taken all the strength from my legs. Don't move, just hold me for a moment longer."

He stroked her back gently. He had no intention of letting her go. "My wife," he said, "my God-given wife. In my dreams, I have held you, only to wake reaching for you as you have escaped me many, many times."

Mericah was still clinging to him. She wanted to disappear into this man of God, where she knew she would be forever safe.

Moses bent over and lifted her off her feet and carried her to his bed. He gently laid her down and knelt at her side. He softly kissed her bare shoulder and whispered into her ear, "My wife, who will be the mother of my children, just being close to you is the answer to a prayer. God has chosen well in you. You shall, one day be fairest of all of heaven's jewels."

Chapter 16

Mariam could not bear the thought of Mericah, an Ethiopian, being lifted up among the family of Leivites. Word spread throughout the tribes that Moses had taken the Ethiopian for his wife. She stirred Aaron against Moses saying, "Did God tell you of this woman? Maybe Moses is mistaken. You should, *we* should tell him that the Lord has said he made a mistake, for I have been told in a dream that she will bring a curse from God upon us."

Aaron was confused by Miriam's words. God had not told him about, nor had he any dreams of, the Ethiopian woman. To this day he had never heard of her from God or Moses. *Maybe she will be a curse to the Hebrews,* he thought. *Maybe this is why the Cushites were so angry; angry enough to tempt us into battle.*

"What has she done against us?" Aaron asked Miriam.

"I warned her and her people to stay away from us or she would be cursed by God. But she's back among us now, as the wife of Moses. She may have used her god to cast a spell upon him and God shall punish us all. Speak with him. Let *us* speak with him before it is to late."

Aaron nodded in agreement.

Chapter 17

Mericah read and put her fingers on the inscribed letters of the stone tablets given to Moses by God. She felt closer to, and some how in touch with, the Almighty; yet, she had trouble interpreting some of the meanings written within the commandments.

She attempted to hold her questions inside so as not to burden Moses. It was not her place, nor the place of mankind to question the gods. But this was not a message from the gods; these were laws conveyed by the God of Abraham. These laws must be understood by all who will live in the land of promise, the land of milk and honey.

Chapter 18

All the tribes of were identified. Each tribe was placed according to its heritage in relation to each of the twelve sons of Jacob. All of the tribes began to adopt the rules; the laws handed down to Moses. Each tribe established its own army and determined its own leadership according to the commands of God and Moses.

The population of the freed Israelites had grown into the millions with Moses and his appointed delegates in charge of keeping the movement of the tribes orderly. God was with the Israelites daily. He guided them by day in a pillar of cloud above and by night from a cloud of fire. The masses of Israelites did not move until God moved, then they followed faithfully."

Most of the Ethiopians had started their journey back to their homeland. Some, though, became a part of the Israelite tribes through marriage, religious commitment or as servants seeking the security of the Most Holy.

Chapter 19

Mericah bore twins. Her two newborn children stayed well within the compounds of the Livites, where she was recognized and respected as not only the wife of Moses, but also as an Ethiopian princess and heir to the throne of Cush. She was surrounded daily by hundreds of her own Ethiopian servants and soldiers, as well as by the holy men and servants of Moses.

Moses himself watched over her and his infant children as often as his duties allowed. He needed her' she was his place of refuge. With her, he was protected from the bombardment of complaints from disgruntled tribesmen and at times, even the pressures of God.

God was, of course, the first to recognize the necessary bond between Moses and Mericah — Moses being God's own chosen author of history and Mericah being the bloodline of the descendants of the historic men of God.

Mericah spent most of her days pondering the lives of both Moses and her new found God of Abraham; she knew very little about either of them. She summoned God daily through prayer and often with an outburst of demands of His presence; only to find, as the angel had told her, 'God would not be at her personal disposal'. Yet, she continued asking questions and demanding some resolution on behalf of her husband, her people and her homelands.

While Moses was away, she and her two children sat directly at the base of the tablets of the commandments and she asked, "Why do you demand that 'we shall not kill', while at this very moment the tribes of Israel are instructed to selectively kill entire villages, 'leaving no stone unturned'?

"How is it that 'we shall have no other God before Thee' when You, our Most Holy, have given gods authority over our lives?

"How shall we resist temptation? How shall my husband not 'covet the presence of another woman' when so many are given unto him as virgins and servants, just as they were to the Pharaoh who took pride in having so many at his feet?

"How shall we 'not bear false witness' for the sake and safety of our own children and loved ones?

"How shall we 'not steal,' when many of our children are overcome with hunger and there are those with plenty that will not share? How will we distinguish what are rightfully the belongings of another or gifts from the gods, when no one stands to claim what is discovered?

"Can my husband clearly define these commandments when You are not present? Can Your commandments be kept by the strongest of us when we are not aware of their purpose? Will we not surely adjust Your meaning to satisfy our own desires and needs? It stands to reason that, at Your hands we most certainly will die. Who shall forgive us when we have been so clearly told what not to do?"

Mericah leaned back for a moment as if waiting for a response to her multitude of questions. Her instincts caused her to resume her search for answers to her questions that, even though it might seem childish or disrespectful. After all, she was a woman who had been taught to question her male counterparts and not to have the audacity to approach a god, let alone the supreme God of Abraham.

Mericah had the courageous heart of an Ethiopian princess. She was one who must know the truths that would enable her to someday become the queen of all the Nile. She possessed the instincts to fairly rule the likes of Moses and the almighty Hebrew nation. She knew she was a spiritual piece of God, and her heart hummed with a feeling of compassion for all of humanity. She was one who once thought she needed to pass through this life before she could be recognized as a descendant of God.

"What, oh Lord, is an adulterer? Is it a king with many wives or a peasant who has gone astray in a moment of fantasy or is it every claimed woman who has tempted a man with submissive eyes or the smell of her inviting perfume? Is adultery an act of sex or is it the desire of one to yield to the overwhelming feelings of lust? Who, among all the world, can meet your expectations? Who will please you, Oh God of Abraham, for only a god can live in a godly manner. We are mere men reaching out to touch a most distant star. We have no choice but to turn from You and rely upon each other for happiness. Is this to be your wish for us?

Chapter 20

Moses summoned Mericah to his place of prayer. When she entered into his presence she immediately realized something had changed. Moses seemed distant.

"Mericah, my princess and mother of my sons, the Lord God Almighty has spoken. The laws of God have been delivered to the twelve sons and tribes of Israel. God's promise to Abraham is being fulfilled. The history of man's beginning is being written and recorded."

Moses paused and turned his back to Mericah and mumbled his next statement. Mericah walked around in front of Moses. She was beginning to become uneasy. The face of Moses had lost its glow and this man doing God's work was not the same. He had a look on his face that Mericah had never seen before. He seemed to have been abandoned by his own confidence. He acted as if all he had hoped for was revealed to have no final solution.

"Vanity," he mumbled. "Even the destiny of the tribes of Israel is shaded with unending disobedience. The Promised Land is not a final place as much as it is another starting point for things to come."

Moses looked into Mericah's eyes and said to her in a voice filled with compassion, "There is no longer a place here for you here. Take my sons and seek a starting place for them. Make a new journey, for my voyage to the Promised Land has just begun and there is no place to write the names of my own children."

"What are you saying?" Mericah asked. "I thought God would be there. Shouldn't we be in the presence of God in the Promised Land, instead on of a journey away from His safety? Don't you want us in God's heaven?"

"God will not be in the Promised Land as a body to look upon or to comfort with daily prayers," Moses said, while again walking away, turning his back to Mericah. "The Promised Land is not a place where God will gather the good and close the gates of the city to those who are not clean. All the world is the Promised Land of God, and in time He will open our eyes and we will find ourselves looking to find a place in God instead of searching high and low for a godly place. I will say no more. Just as you left Egypt, you must now leave this place and seek the way of God."

Mericah grabbed this arm and pulled him around to face her. "What do you mean, Moses?" she asked. Mericah trembled as she realized that Moses had already begun putting distance between himself and her.

"Why are you killing me and your sons?" she asked, "No! We will not leave! We are going with you. I want to stay with God," she said while trying to put her arms around Moses.

Moses immediately pushed her away. He had made up his mind or perhaps his mind was made up for him.

"Please," Mericah whispered, to no avail, as Moses freed himself and summoned Joshua.

"All Ethiopians, Nubians and others who are not Hebrews, can no longer remain with the people of Israel. They must prepare themselves to leave before the new moon. I have spoken the Word of God, which shall not be questioned," Moses said, then went off into seclusion for prayer.

Mericah sadly watched as her man walked away. *He won't really leave his children or me,* she thought desperately, as he continued to walk off out of sight.

"All right!" she screamed as loud as she could. "We will leave this place and find our own God. We will never forgive this act of abandonment by you and your people. Our new god will make us a mighty race," she vowed, and your sons will find favor in a good and kind god."

She fell to her knees in anguish, "Why, God, why have you turned your back on us? Why has Moses so quickly forgotten his love for us?" Mericah lay motionless where Moses left her. She was heartbroken and had no will to stand. She lay completely limp and decided she would die right there, without another word or thought. She refused to take air into her lungs. She would not open her eyes. She tried to stop her heart from beating, only to find it beating harder and louder than ever before.

"Rise up! Rise up and live!"

Mericah slightly opened her eyes to see who was interrupting her death wish, but she saw no one.

"What will become of your children? Where is the spirited woman who questioned the likes of God and the voices of His servants? Is she lying in defeat?"

"I feel so helpless and lost," Mericah said. "I can't lift myself up, I have no God, no place to take my children and we have lost the love of Moses."

"Moses has done what is best for you, your children and your people. He has obeyed God even though it pains him more than you will ever know. Rise up and find your way for the sake of all those who will come after you. For your children, who are descendants of God, and for God who admires your courage and your will to survive. Be on your way, for He has a place prepared for you."

Chapter 21

The proclamation of Moses was quickly spread among the non-Hebrew races. The Ethiopians were divided about the possible consequences of being separated from the powerful forces of the God-led armies of Israel. The chances of successfully retreating across the Red Sea and south into Nubia were very slim now that the entire Egyptian nation and her allies were working to restore the Pharaoh and the life they had become so accustomed to.

The Nubians were waging war against the Pharaoh on the southern borders of Egypt, but with very little success. The advancement northward was much too slow to connect their warring forces with the now to be exiled forces containing Mericah and their Egyptian-trained elite warriors.

The Egyptians easily dominated the encounters in the flat desert areas with their superior chariots and horsemen. The forces of Nubians and their allies from the south were relentlessly battling, literally inch by inch. They were not equipped to overrun the Egyptians with their retreat and attack-type war tactics.

The Nubian's mighty foot soldiers and spearmen tried again and again to slow the speed and agility of the Egyptian chariots and horsemen, but to no avail. The thousands and thousands of black soldiers were often fighting without a clear motive; most were unaware of boundaries and stone riches.

Some had heard of the quest for the stone gods and the abundance of food and crops that would come by way of those they captured. Others believed if they did not fight, then the gods of the Pharaoh would take away all of their lands and their children would be sent to serve the warlike Pharaoh of the north. Nonetheless, they fought bravely and were willing to give up their lives for the advancement of fellow soldiers behind them.

The Nubians and Ethiopians, in general, were a tall, lean, muscular people who had the ability to go for days without eating or drinking. Their past had taught them to preserve selected dried roots and fruit seeds that could be easily carried and consumed for a needed burst of energy during hunts or during long droughts.

Most of their preferred food grew along the Nile River and for generation's rumors were passed on about the rich, fertile, marshlands where the Nile emptied into the flat lands of Egypt, where there was a bountiful source of their preferred foods. They thought there would be rewards for those who fought hard enough to defeat the enemy and reach a Promised Land of their own.

Then, of course, there was all of Africa's knowledge of the captured Ethiopian Queen, Mericah. She was rumored to be the most beautiful black woman who had ever lived. It was believed that she had been put on earth for the third time. This third life was believed to be the final test for mankind to provide a perfect bride for the god of abundance. Because of her, all the people of Africa would attain unending happiness when the marriage was complete.

The Ethiopians were wrongly convinced that the Pharaoh was the god of choice and that the new world would be at hand when the Pharaoh transposed himself from man to god. Realizing that they had been deceived, all the kings of Nubia and Ethiopia vowed to bring her back to await the coming of the true god of abundance. Without her, they believed that god would not bless them, and would instead burden them with three thousand years of hardship and servitude.

Chapter 22

On land, Mohab was a geographical genius. He was well aware of the locations of the enemies of the African races. He was well deserving of his previous position with the Pharaoh's army as their number-one strategic officer.

His obligation to return Mericah to the homeland was his purpose in life. The time of truth had finally arrived. Mericah becoming pregnant by Moses had confused Mohab and now she wanted to be taken back to the homeland and away from the masses of Hebrews who were bound for the Promised Land. Mericah and her twin sons by Moses must survive in spite of the Pharaoh and of Moses.

Mohab decided to make an attempt to avoid a frontal battle with the main Egyptian army. He headed north, following the riverbed of the river Egypt, which at this time of year carries little or no water. This tactic would let his mounted soldiers protect the flanks of his still formidable foot soldiers and spearmen, by always being positioned on higher ground. His forces would also be divided into three bodies, with the center body of soldiers on the perimeter of Mericah and the women and children.

Although some were reluctant to leave the safety afforded by Moses, the choice was not theirs. Within weeks, the Nubians and Ethiopians were organized and prepared to leave for their new destination under the leadership of Mohab.

Moses directed that they be given provisions equal to those of his own tribes. As the parting of the masses began, Moses personally came to bless the journey of those who had been in bondage with his people for so long.

Mohab and Moses exchanged wishes of well being to one another, hugged each other in a manly way and bid a final farewell.

As Mericah prepared the twins for the departure, the area outside her tent suddenly became silent. As she walked toward the tent opening to see what was going on, Moses pulled the tarp aside and stepped in. With head held high in a proud way he extended his hands to Mericah.

"Mericah," he said quietly, "you and my sons are the reason for my being. Before you, this man did not truly exist. But God is a mighty and demanding God who is never without purpose. If only you and I had been chosen as grains of sand, we would have been inseparable. Instead we were chosen as pillars that are the foundation of which neither can exist without us. We are now a left and a right that cannot be brought together. All of heaven weeps and wishes for the healing of your heart. I can only pray that the weight of the burdens of my own heart could be lifted long enough that I may, as a man, fulfill my obligations to God and at the same time worship my earthly princess.

"The choice to defy God or to defy myself and seek the comfort of my woman's love, leaves me with no choice. God has given me a moment with you, which I value more than a lifetime of pleasures. Now we are being separated for the sake of a nation under God," Moses lowered his head and his voice and made a welcoming gesture for Mericah to come into his open arms.

Without hesitation, Mericah stepped forward, forgave him and rested her head upon his chest. This time Moses felt weak in the knees, and his tears found their way to the surface. He drew in a deep breath and held Mericah at arm's length.

"Love seems to have no place when a man or woman is on a mission for God," he said, while looking directly into her eyes. "Please hold in your heart a sacred place for us, despite what the heavens have demanded." Then he whispered, "I love you." With those final words, he released her and turned to depart.

Mericah knew that she and her two sons would never see him again. Yet she knew that even though he had just turned and walked away, he had left her his soul and they would never part. Mericah understood. "Farewell," she whispered.

Mericah had been with Moses for nearly three years. She was with him immediately after the exodus until their parting at Kadesh.

Chapter 23

The Egyptians, in pursuit of the Hebrews, had blocked any possible exit through the Sea of Reeds or the southern shores that might have proved a way back to Ethiopia by ship. The Nubians, Ethiopians and all the non-Hebrew races headed north.

Knowing that the river Egypt would lead them to the sea, they began the slow journey to what they thought would be the safest way back home. Mohab's final plan was to take the well guarded city of Gaza by surprise and seize as many seaworthy ships as possible to carry them westward past northern Egypt to the shoreline of northwest Nubia. From there, they would journey southeast into the homelands.

Mohab had reports that the people of Nephilirn were giants and more than formidable foes for any army of the world. Mohab had a plan of attack to defeat them.

With Moses and the Israelites now far southeast and confronting obstacles and foes of their own, Mohab's army finally reached the divide of the river Egypt. At the break of day, Mohab prepared his fighting men for battle.

He walked back and forth in front of eight of his most trusted Ethiopian and Nubian warriors. "Willingness," he said. "We must be willing to kill and perhaps die for what we believe in. We must pursue the destiny that has long been embedded into the people of Cush. To quit is not an option. To lie down and rest is not an option. To hesitate to strike is not an option.

"Our warriors must attack relentlessly. They must be assured that if they are fortunate enough to lose their lives in battle, they will live as kings for eternity. For every enemy slain, they will be given riches. For every battle we win, they will receive praise from all their forefathers. For the destruction of the Egyptian army, we will receive many wives and become kings of our own lands.

"The lands and riches of eternity are vast and the gods have prepared a special place for all who have lived and died bravely. For, all of the gods await the return of our queen to her rightful place. Until then, there can be no happiness at home. Until then, the gods cannot return from stone to flesh and the dead shall remain dead."

Mohab's mind was racing with doubt as he spoke to his leaders. All he had been taught from childhood until the exodus was now clouded by his recent experiences, including the parting of the Red sea, Manna from the heavens, and the many other miracles of Moses. The overwhelming new belief that one Almighty God exist over all others, and this God's command that, "Thou shall have no other god before Me," began to overwhelm his mind.

The men stood waiting patiently for Mohab to finalize his instructions. Mohab, after a long pause, gazed at his men from left to right. He thought of what the black female on the roadside said. He thought again of the Egyptians being swallowed by the Red Sea at the command of Moses.

Fear found its way into Mohab's mind. He began to wonder, *What if the God of Moses is with the enemy? What if the roadside angel was wrong and not strong enough to protect his army? What if my acts lead to the recapture or the death of Mericah and the sons of Moses?* Strangely, he wanted to pray just as he had seen Moses and Aaron pray.

At first he stuttered, "Oh, God ... Oh, Mighty God ...." The eight warriors immediately looked at Mohab, wondering what he was trying to say. He had just told them the gods' expectations and now he was praying without the presence of a stone or golden god.

They stepped back as Mohab fell upon his knees and looked to the heavens. "Oh, mighty God of Moses, please be with us. We now deliver our nation into your hands. In the face of our enemy, we ask that you be with us as you were with the Hebrew nation as they left Egypt."

Six or the eight warriors backed farther away and left their leader. They feared the gods would destroy Mohab as he knelt in prayer to a foreign god. The remaining two warriors remained with Mohab as he continued, "We ask that Your spirit be with us and give us the strength of the same winds that blew and divided the Red Sea. We give our trust and loyalty to You, God of Moses, that You may lead us home safely."

One of the remaining two warriors broke his silence and scorned Mohab for his abandonment of the gods. "Shame!" he said. "It is a shame that a warrior of Ethiopia goes to his knees to worship with prayer a god we cannot see. Look, there is nothing up there. I have the notion to strike you dead," he added, while putting his hand on his sword.

The last remaining warrior quickly drew his own sword and put his fellow officer to death with one hard thrust through his heart.

Mohab paused, as the body of one of his warriors slumped forward and fell against his thigh. Mohab looked at the slain Ethiopian and then for the first time he folded his hands together in the manner he had seen Moses do. He slowly raised them far above his head. But, before he could speak again, the black female from the roadside appeared at the side of the remaining warrior.

"Where is your faith Mohab?" she asked. "Surely you know there is only one true God. Though he has many voices and has been called by many names, He is still the One that other gods fear."

Mohab and his warrior comrade both fell in fear with their faces against the ground. They knew they were in the presence of a messenger of God

"Have we prayed without the permission of the most powerful?" Mohab asked. "We are sorry."

"You have only to pray from your soul to be heard by God. He is aware of your plight and He will show you the way. He will wait while your children's children go astray again and again, until like you, they recognize His voice among the voices of thousands of gods. He will welcome them as your father welcomed you.

"Do not make war against the giants, for they are preparing for Moses. Ask, and they shall assist you into the sea without bloodshed. Your numbers will now be less than a thousand and your journey will be long and natural. God will not be at your calling during your journey, for fate must have its share of life and its share of the lives of the earthly seeds of the Almighty.

"Lift yourselves up and take your remaining people forward, for the others have left you and are headed into Egypt to do battle. Surely, their gods of stone will not welcome you or the sons of Moses home again. They will say 'you have been with the Hebrew God of Abraham, of whom they have forgotten'; yet, they will have their place in God's heart." With that, just as quickly as she had come, she had vanished from view.

Mohab and his warrior slowly peered upward and all around before standing up. Their swords were gone, along with the body of their slain comrade.

Chapter 24

At daybreak on the river Egypt the air was hot and dry. By high noon, the sandy ground was scorching hot. The soles of the feet of the nearly one thousand Ethiopians had become calloused like leather; yet, they continued north. Most of them followed Mohab in hope of finding their homelands and their families; they had long been separated. Others wanted to stay near Mericah, feeling somehow, she would lead them to God.

They caravanned toward the great Mediterranean Sea, and despite the heat, despite hunger, despite the feeling of being lost, they hummed songs of their homeland. The sounds of the hummed music seemed to bounce off every sand dune, causing a feeling that the gods had joined in on the music as a gesture that they were pleased with these humble people. So they hummed, sometimes from morning to night, often without a word being spoken.

When the sun fell beyond the horizon, they huddled together in groups and slept soundly under the wings of God. Each night, Mohab went ahead of the caravan and bowed down on his knees to pray. "God of Moses," he would say, "we know you are watching over us. Just as the wandering herds of our homeland, we blindly walk in faith, unwilling to lead ourselves and unwilling to determine our own direction."

The nightly sounds of the wild were frightening, but inside the perimeters of the Ethiopians, there was no sound. While the stars glittered in the jet-black sky and the moon hung quietly overhead, sleep became an anticipated and desired pleasure.

Mericah often lay awake, gently stroking the heads of her two boys. She watched the sky as the heat of the day rose above the land caused the stars to dance.

> *"Rejoice, oh heaven, for soon all will be well. Soon heaven and earth will marry and our child will be called the Son of God. He will bring gentleness to every life and to every soul."*

After many days and nights had gone by, the Ethiopians awakened to an unusually quiet morning and the startling sight of thousands of armed men surrounding their campsite. These were huge men, most of them seven feet tall. They were mounted on horses more than twice the size of those the Ethiopians had come to know.

These giant men were posed as if ready for battle, but they made no aggressive moves toward the Ethiopians. The Ethiopian warriors held fast their swords and spears as they stood without fear, largely outnumbered but instinctively poised to protect themselves even from these giants among men.

"Greetings," said one of the giant horsemen. "Why are you in our land and from where have you come?"

"We are Ethiopians, making our way back to our own lands Mohab responded. "We have no quarrel with you. We only wish to pass through peacefully."

"What will you pay for passage through our land?" asked another giant that was dressed in a hard leather breastplate and mask.

"We have the finest spears and swords in all of northern Africa. We wish to trade them for tools needed to build ships for our journey dictated and protected in the safety of the God of Abraham," Mohab answered.

"God of Abraham you say"?

"Yes," said Mohab.

The giant horsemen rode off briefly and three other horsemen returned. One appeared to be a leader.

"Greetings, black man," one of the new horseman said. "Are you from the tribe of Abraham?"

"I cannot answer that," said Mohab. "We are Ethiopians who have been directed by the God of Abraham to ask your people for safe passage to the sea."

The giant horseman and three others rode their horses up close to Mohab, directly into the midst of the Ethiopians. They had mistakenly thought that this was a group of slaves. He looked into the eyes of Mohab and then he looked into the face of Mericah, who was standing nearby.

"Are you fleeing the Pharaoh of Egypt?" he asked.

"We have left the Pharaoh, but we flee from no one."

The Giant continued speaking to Mohab, while not taking his eyes off Mericah. "Are you enemy or friend of the Egyptians?"

"Neither," answered Mohab. We have chosen to not be an enemy of anyone and we know that the Pharaoh is not worthy of a friendship.

"Who is the woman that appears so easy on the eyes?" asked the lead horseman.

"She is my sister," said Mohab.

"I am Mericah of Ethiopia," Mericah responded on her own behalf. "Who may I ask are you?"

The horseman did not answer right away; instead he rode closer to Mericah. The Ethiopian warriors drew their swords, as the horseman approached her. Four black men positioned themselves between the approaching horseman and Mericah.

"I see she is worthy of your lives," said the horseman.

"Assist us and we shall spare the lives of many of your men," Mericah boldly said.

The horseman paused, for he was taken aback by the courage and seemingly foolish statement spoken by the woman. "You, with so few, would rise up and strike against us? That would surely mean your death in a matter of minutes," said the horseman.

"Perhaps," said Mericah. "But you will surely be the first to die, for you have blundered into the midst of brave fighting men. You and your men are big, and your hearts are easy targets for our spearmen."

Mericah had challenged the horseman to see if he was willing to die. She sensed that the brave but foolish horseman was an important member of this army of giants.

"We have not come to shed blood, we have come at the direction of our God, who has seen fit to render even Pharaoh powerless against us. What chance have you against that? You are mere men," Mericah continued.

The horseman looked around and realized he and his three comrades, while talking to Mohab and Mericah, had unintentionally put themselves dangerously deep into the ranks of the Ethiopians.

Mohab noticed that three of the horseman wore battered and torn armor; their feet and sandals were dirty. Their clothing was stained with blood, as if they had previously been in many battles. One of the men, though, wore armor was finely polished and the sword and emblem hanging around his neck was studded with jewels and trimmed with gold. This one had not yet spoken, but he nodded to the horseman asking the questions, as if to signal him to go on.

Mohab made his way closer to the bejeweled horseman, without being noticed as they continued their talks with Mericah.

"Do you possess gold or jewels?" the horseman asked while simply ignoring Mericah's threat. "It is said that Numbia and Ethiopia are rich with precious stones and they are your primary bargaining tools with Pharaoh. Do you have gold with you now, my black beauty?" he asked, while slowly trying to ease his way back toward his own soldiers and out of the group of black warriors.

"Yes," answered Mericah. "We have gold and we are willing to trade for your assistance and materials to build three ships that can carry our people back to the Nubian shores."

"What is to stop us from killing all of you and taking your possessions? You have trespassed into our territory and it is our right." the horseman said

"For the reason that I have just stated. You and many of your soldiers will die, and God will see us through," she answered.

The horseman was getting nervous and his indecision caused his horse to prance in place. He turned and looked toward the bejeweled horseman for some indication of what to do next. Then he turned his horse once more toward Mericah and momentarily raised himself up out of his saddle. He looked toward his waiting army of men, and had just begun to raise his arm, when Mohab grabbed the jeweled horseman and pulled him to the ground, quickly placing his sword against the man's neck.

"Wait! "the horseman shouted. "Don't kill him; let us talk."

"Tell your men to back off, completely out of sight, or I will cut off his head," Mohab said while pressing his foot hard against the chest of the bejeweled horseman.

The man waved his hand and signaled his army to disperse. A voice within the horsemen's forces called out, "They have the price and are threatening to kill him. Do as they say or the king will have our heads. Back up!"

Reluctantly the forces began to slowly back away, leaving the prince and his three soldiers captive among the Ethiopians.

"Get down off of your horses," Mohab commanded, Get down now, or your prince is dead."

"Don't be foolish. We can work this out," the horseman said.

Mericah watched as the men on both sides became still. Mohab stood with the helpless prince at his feet, as armed warriors surrounded the remaining horsemen. The Nephilim armies were moving away in confusion.

"Help the prince stand up," said Mericah.

Mohab pulled the huge man to his feet, keeping his sword close to his throat.

"Listen my friend," Mericah said in a kind voice, "we mean you and your people no harm. Please, let us pass through your land in peace. We will gladly trade our goods in exchange for the supplies we need. Give me your word that we can trade as neighbors, and my brother will put down his sword."

The prince nodded in agreement and Mohab put his sword away. The prince rubbed his throat realizing that he had come very close to losing his life. He finally regained his composure and removed his mask. He was a young man, though his size appeared much too big for his boyish face.

"You have put me in an awkward position," he said." We are the most feared army in the whole region and I have foolishly fallen into the hands of a black army led by a woman. You give me no choice but to cooperate. What have you to offer in exchange for our help."

"We will give you a chest of gold in exchange for use of three ships with crews to take us west of Egypt," Mericah said.

"What about swords? You said you would trade swords and spears, the prince asked.

"If your armies will escort us to the sea and protect us from the Egyptians, we will give you spears, but the men will not give up their swords," Mohab said.

"Where is the gold? asked the prince.

"The gold is not with the caravan, but is carried and protected by our scouts who are hidden not far from here," answered Mohab.

Mericah directed someone to bring a small token of proof to show the quality of gold that was to be traded. As the gold was brought forth, she said, "Here, this is what we have to offer." She handed the huge young prince a small leather pouch filled with gold trinkets that had formerly been used as items of worship.

"We have no need for gold," she said. We only wish to go home."

The prince's eyes sparkled as he pulled his gold filled hand from the pouch. He knew his father would be pleased with the procurement of such valuables. "When will we receive the rest?" asked the prince.

"When we set sail, we will signal our scouts to bring a chest filled with riches," Mericah said.

The prince nodded to his soldiers and sent one of them to tell his forces to head west of the caravan toward Egypt. They were to kill anyone who approached the Ethiopians, who were now considered friends.

Chapter 25

The Nephilim horsemen led the Ethiopians out of the riverbed and Northeast into Southern Gaza. There, they exchanged a chest of gold for three ships big enough to carry more than a thousand tribesmen, women and children.

The Ethiopians were welcomed with opened arms at Gaza. Mohab traded with the Cannanites and the Nephilim warriors and obtained additional food and other goods they would need for their journey.

While her people performed their final preparations, Mericah took her two boys and walked along the shores of the great sea. She yearned to speak to Moses. She yearned for one more chance to say goodbye.

She still feared that without Moses, she would have no access to God. Without God, she had no way to convince the people of her homelands to give up their tribal laws and customs to pursue the One True God.

Though she no longer had the tablets with the laws on them, the words were written in her heart. These new laws of Moses had been the laws of her land since time began, but without access to God, she feared that her people, like the Israelites, would revert to the stone gods of Egypt.

She wondered again and again if God would come to her land once Moses and the Israelites were secure in the Promised Land. She also wondered how often she should pray and how was she would know when God was present to hear her prayer. After all, this was the God of Moses, how could he have time to hear anyone else when the Israelites were so many.

She had learned that the Hebrews had little or no faith in the God that brought them from the grip of the Pharaoh. How long would it be before God came to Ethiopia?

Mohab quietly walked up behind her. "Mericah, we will be at sea tomorrow. I just wanted to ask you if you thought that the God of Moses will hear us if we pray to Him while we are at sea."

"I don't know," she answered. "I don't think so, but we must not, under any circumstances, summon any other god. If we have learned anything, it is that God hates the gods of Egypt."

"Our people are excited about the prospect of finally reaching home," Mohab said. "Will we be welcomed? Will our father understand the power of the God of Moses? He has not seen it with his own eyes, as we have. He may not recognize a God that he cannot see. He might be like my fellow warriors, who left us. Will he disown us or call us fools?"

"I feel within my heart, that somehow God watches over us."

"Will he help us? I'm not sure," she answered her own question and then continued to speak. "Somehow, I believe His eyes are among the stars, and He is able to see all that we do. His ears are among the birds and bees and He hears all that we say. I feel His spirit is within our hearts and He feels all that we feel. Yet I, too, wonder if He hungers with us. Does He feel our fears or our pain of uncertainty? I just don't know. I must have faith that He has a place for us."

Mohab looked into his sister's eyes and found a small sense of reassurance there. "Maybe," he said. "Maybe God will see us through this journey at sea."

Just after daybreak, the Ethiopians filed onto the waiting ships. Within hours, they were all aboard and headed out to sea.

Chapter 26

They sailed westward as close to the shoreline as the stony shore would allow. After three days, most of the Ethiopians became ill. The constant motion of the sea caused everyone but the Cananite captain and his shipmates to wish for death rather than this never before experienced seasickness. Many believed that they had been cursed and would be forced to live this way into eternity.

On the third night, everyone aboard the ships fell into a deep sleep. The ships continued westward, with no one at the helms. After many days, those aboard the ships began to wake. They had no idea how long they had been asleep, but it was obvious they had sailed into unfamiliar waters.

There was no land in sight in any direction. The sea was calm, though the sails were full and carrying the ships along at an unheard of pace.

Mericah was awakened by the ship's captain, who was concerned that she might still be ill. "Where are we?" she asked. "Are we nearer to our destination?"

"I have no idea where we are or how the crews and I fell asleep for so long. You can see the other two ships, one in front of us and one to our rear, but there is no land in sight. We have lost our direction, but I believe we will see a shoreline soon."

Days passed, and there was still no land in sight. No one aboard knew how long they had been at sea. The captain, fearful of not being able to correct his navigation, decided to turn around and head back to Gaza.

Another week passed, and the captain of the lead ship had changed course more than three times in an attempt to find the land of northern Africa. Water and food supplies were dwindling and a new reign of fear was setting on the people.

Chapter 27

We are doomed, thought Mohab, *I have led my people to their doom. Anything, I would do anything to feel the earth under my feet again. I would take on the entire Egyptian army rather than die at sea. No one at home will know what has become of us. No one will know if we died bravely at the hands of gods or man.*

"Do you think we should pray?" Mericah asked the captain.

"I don't know. How could any god hear us out here?"

"I will pray to God, He will lead us to shore," Mericah said confidently. As she began to pray, the sea began to stir, causing the ships to rise and fall with each wave.

"Hold on to something," the crewmen shouted. The ships were suddenly rocked from side to side and began taking on water with each splashing wave.

Mericah, now clutching her two boys with one arm and holding on with the other, had not yet began to pray. The words just wouldn't come. She had abandoned God and reverted to pure and natural fear; the type of fear that causes a man to grasp for any within his reach.

The rising and falling of the ship caused Mericah and her children to slam hard onto the ship's deck with each drop. The children were crying, but still clinging to their mother's clothing. The ship rocked again and again, causing one of the boys to be torn away from his mother and brother. The ship tilted nearly on its side, and the young boy slid quickly to the opposite side of the ship before hitting the side railing.

Mericah screamed at the sight of her child headed toward the water, while she clung to her other child. She watched as her baby looked back at her one last time, his pleading eyes cried for help the as the sea came aboard and ruthlessly swallowed him.

Again the ship slammed against the sea, and again her body slammed hard against the deck of the ship. The ship twisted and slung the second child from her grasp. The child was frantically reaching for his mother when the ship tilted onto one side and then whipped back to the other. All around, people were being thrown about like wet rags; back and forth they slammed into rails and fixtures and then hard against the deck.

Mericah's second child slid down toward the outer rail of the ship. She watched helplessly as the same angry sea waited to inhale her remaining baby. She released her grasp and quickly crawled toward her child, who was now hanging onto a piece of railing for his dear life.

"No!" Mericah screamed as she was swept in another direction away from her child. The ship reared upward again, causing the boy to lose his grasp and slide toward the center of the ship. For a split second, the ship leveled off long enough for Mericah to stand and run to her child, only to lose him again. Fatigued and frustrated, Mericah reached out toward her child as he slid towards the rail where his brother had gone overboard. She was too far away.

"No!" she screamed as he, too, looked back at his mother while crying and trying to grab anything he could to halt the slide. Just as the ship tilted for one more bucking throw, the captain came from out of nowhere and ran toward the child. He slammed his huge body over the child, causing both of them to slide against the outer railing. The captain's mighty grip had latched onto a sturdy rail, but both of their bodies were slung into the sea. All Mericah could see was the captain's wet fist wrapped around the one rail that was still holding fast.

Just as quickly as it started, the storm began to subside. With the ship still rocking, Mericah stood and ran toward the captain and her child.

The captain pulled himself up onto the ship's deck, and her child was not in his arms.

"No! No! No! she cried out, just as the captain pulled his legs up onto the ship with the limp body of the child squeezed tightly between them. The rocking of the ship ceased as the wind and rain suddenly passed.

Mericah fell to her child and pulled his body into her breast. "Please, God, Almighty God, don't take my baby."

The child began coughing while spitting water. Not far away, the captain lay flat on his back, as the dark clouds moved off like they were hastily looking for other victims to destroy.

The captain turned and watched as the young boy began to cry again, while clinging to his mother. Mericah frantically looked out into the sea, searching for Nemiah, her other son. She hoped and prayed that somehow he had survived, but he was gone, swallowed by the cruel and natural sea.

There was no trace of him, only the waves of the sea and the dark clouds in the distance. Mericah was stricken with sadness as she finally stopped looking and sat down with her surviving child cradled on her lap.

"Why?" she asked. "Why have you taken my baby?"

Chapter 28

Where there had been three ships carrying more than a thousand people and the two precious children of Moses, now there are two broken and damaged ships and one child of Moses. They were still lost at sea, and the wailing and crying of so many sent an eerie message into the heavens.

"Where are you, God? Where is Your mighty hand? Which of the gods of Egypt has overpowered You? Which god has taken so many from us?"

Back on the second ship, Mohab, like everyone else, had clung to whatever was sound enough to hold his weight. The second ship had been tossed and tumbled just like the first. Mohab's ship contained four hundred people, three hundred of them warriors. Mericah's contained three hundred and forty people, mostly women and children, and was considered the most seaworthy of the three. Its captain was the most experienced and was the leader of this small fleet. The third ship carried a little more than two hundred, along with most of the extra cargo being taken back to the homeland.

Once Mohab's ship settled back into its upright position, he moved toward the bow in search of the other ships, but none were in sight. He ran from one side of the ship to the other, trying to spot Mericah's ship.

He saw nothing but open sea and off in the distance, the lightning and wind-driven storm that had just moments ago released them from it's grasp.

Again and again, he ran back and forth, looking and searching, but there were no other ships. "My God! he screamed, while looking to the heavens. "What have you done? Have You brought us this far just to rip the heart out of us with disaster. What have You done?" he screamed again in anger.

Mohab drew his sword and violently swung in every direction. Side to side he swung into thin air; he thrust and stabbed downward, upward and every which way, like a mad man. "I will kill you!" he shouted. "I will kill you, God of Moses, for You have deceived us. You have taken away every hope we had." He raised his sword above his head and swung as if to slice the clouds that were far out of his reach. He swung ... and swung and swung ... until he fell exhausted on the ship's deck.

Still, he screamed until his voice became faint. "I will kill you, God! I will take Your life as you have taken the lives of so many." All of the warriors who had gathered around watched, as their leader passed into unconsciousness with the words, "I'll kill you," still being muttered.

Three of the soldiers lifted their leader from the deck and put him atop a pile of linens where he slept. Everyone on the ship was saddened by the sight of such a strong man falling in despair at the feet of this new God. They were, all of them, quiet and as humble as a man could get; yet, they were afraid that this and every journey had now come to an end.

They thought, *This must surely be the end of the world. We must have chosen the wrong god.*

Chapter 29

As the sea became calm and the sun above their ships was shining brightly, the horizon was dark in every direction, and the storm had just begun...

The captain of the ship Mericah was aboard recalled hearing of storms at sea such as the one they had just experienced. These powerful storms were known to happen off of the western coast of Nubia. Stories were told about the huge storms that came on suddenly and swept many ships westward. The stories always told of how the storm would end with an eerie calm and after a short while would start up again much stronger and more treacherous that before. Most of the ships caught in these storms were never heard from again.

The captain began to instruct his men to tie everyone to solid parts of the ship's mast and other sturdy fixtures.

"But sir, the storm has ended and the sun is shining brightly," one of the shipmates said.

"The horizon is dark in every direction," the captain responded. "I have heard of these storms and we are much further out to sea than we thought. These storms are said to strike twice, with the worst being the second half. Get everyone secure and prepare for more rough seas and strong winds," the captain said.

"Where are the other ships?" asked Mericah, as the captain approached to instruct her that the storm had not ended and everyone must secure themselves.

"I don't know," he answered. "The lookouts are stationed and on watch, but as of yet, none of the other ships have been spotted. I guess we must assume that they are lost."

Mericah secured Ariah, her remaining son, to a wooden post with strips of linen. She didn't want to lose her second son to the demon-like seas. She then tied herself to the same post. She looked out to sea; looking for her brother, whom she had learned to love since their meeting in Egypt.

She was suffering deeply from despair from the lost of Nemiah. The very thought of her baby drowning at sea caused her more pain than any human should bear. Now she had lost her brother, too. How can any woman carry so much sadness and still want to live.

"Where are you Moses? Why aren't you here with all your godly powers? How much more grief will your God cause us? I have done nothing to deserve your vengeance, oh God of Moses. I will not give up, no matter what you take from me. I will cling to life until my last breath. I have asked, I have begged for the life of my child who was ripped from my grasp by the sea. I can only hope that my brother, my child and my people who have died are now with you in the heavens like Moses has spoken so strongly of."

Chapter 30

The captain was right, and the storm was back. The ship began to violently rock and sway just as before. As it was tossed into the night, Mericah's sanity found refuge in sleep.

"Moses," she said in her dream, "I see you my dearest. I knew you would come. Is that Nemiah you are carrying? I'm so relieved you are here. How is it that you are walking on the sea? Is that God with you?

"I'm sorry, God. I'm sorry that I lost faith in You. I should have known you wouldn't let us suffer. Where is Mohab? Is he with you? Yes, I see him. How is it that he can ride his horse upon the sea? He's so gallant and proud, I knew he would never be defeated by the sea. He's much too strong for that.

"Give me my baby. Oh Nemiah, mother was so sick without you, my precious child. Come to me.

"Is that Ethiopia? There, over there, off to your right. It is! Home! We are home. Mother and Father are waving to us. I'm so happy now. Thank you God for being so kind. I will never doubt you again. I will be the fairest of all of the queens of Ethiopia and of all of the lands of Nubia. With You, God, we will have everything and all will be well in our land that worships the only true God."

"Mericah," the captain softly said. "Mericah, wake up. The storm has ended," he said while untying Ariah.

"Here is some water. Drink it sparingly, we do not know how long our water supply will last."

"Where did they go?" Mericah asked as she began to come to the realization that all she had seen was just a dream.

"Where did who go?" asked the captain.

"God, Moses, Nemiah, Mohab," said Mericah.

"They're not here, Mericah," said the captain.

Mericah's heart fell. She felt faint and collapsed as she was trying to stand. Ariah began to cry and climbed into Mericah's arms, as she lay there barely conscious. "Its' all right, my love. Mother is all right," Mericah said, and hugged Ariah tight.

"For you," she said, "For you I will live, you will be my hope. You will be the beginning of my life. For yo, baby, just for you.

Chapter 31

Unlike the captain of Mericah's ship, the captain of the ship that carried Mohab did not prepare for the second devastating storm. Mohab convinced himself that some evil god that had taken Mericah had returned to take his life and the lives of his remaining warriors. This time he did not draw his sword, for he now realized he had accused the God of Moses and even wished to slay Him. When in truth, in his heart, he knew that the God of Moses was not a killer of good men and women. He knew that the God of Moses was a protective and just God. He concluded that he had led his sister and his people away from the land of the One and only true and caring God.

"If God could hear me," he said out loud, "I would say I'm sorry. I blamed God, just as many men before me have looked to blame the Almighty for our own shortcomings and errors."

He began to pray, "Forgive me, God Almighty, I again have displayed my nature as just a man. If you can hear my voice from afar, I pray to you, first for the forgiveness of my constant blindness; secondly, for my foolish acts of faithlessness. Most of all, I ask your forgiveness and your mercy on behalf of all the black races who have unknowingly followed the ways of the idol and stone worshipers of the north."

Mohab continued to pray, "Now that this storm is again upon us, waiting to deliver it's evil and final blow, I pray that You take us to Your kingdom and let us join with our ancestors and our people of pure and humble hearts. Now I know that all is not lost at the end of this life. How could anything be lost when we have found God? If You can hear me, God, I beg of You, let Your will be done, that we can be with You together in eternal happiness."

The storm delivered its surging waves and destructive winds, and yet there were no more deaths.

Chapter 32

As the morning sun appeared in the east at the beginning of the sea, Mohab was awakened by one of his comrades. "Mohab, there is a ship on the horizon. The captain believes it is one of ours."

Mohab leaped to his feet. "God Almighty, please let it be Mericah!"

As both ships steered toward each other, the anticipation from both Mohab and Mericah was building up at a heart-bursting pace. Finally, the ships were close enough to be recognized. Like an answer to a prayer, the brother and sister spotted each other, and Mericah was in tears again but this time they were tears of joy.

Mohab leaped up and down like a child, "My sister, our princess has come back alive!" he shouted, "God has blessed us!"

After the reunion of the two remaining ships, Mohab and the two captains decided to sail with the wind until they came to land. The sea remained choppy for several days, but the winds following the storm were strong enough to keep the sails filled. They traveled many miles swiftly on the open sea without incident.

They had the strong winds at their backs and prayed for thirty days. They were alive, but they were still lost, afraid and running low on drinking water. No matter what, though, here would be no giving up.

Mericah spent most of her time gazing out at the sea at this point. She was always wishing and wondering about Moses. In her heart, she still felt that by some miracle she would see both Moses and Nemiah again. After all, this new God had no boundaries. There was nothing He couldn't do.

She was no longer the child who left Egypt. She was now a princess, soon to be queen. She still remained inquisitive and yet, due to many recent experiences in such a short time, she was satisfied with one fact — the fact that God and fate were in control of hers and everyone else's lives.

Even though she knew she could not possibly understand God's reasoning or fate's randomness, she could not stop asking why ... Why? ... Why? She hungered for answers with every breath she took. When someone looked upon her, they would first see her beauty and if they were bold enough to stare for a few seconds, they would see the face of a woman with questions hidden behind the very essence of her partial smile.

Some of the Ethiopians believed that if they were to gaze at her beauty too long, their souls would wander forever in love and no other face could take the place of the vision of Mericah. They thought a man could literally die of starvation due to his lust and yearning to touch her. Her beauty was haunting ... her brilliance head and shoulder above the wisest of men. She was a goddess waiting to be acknowledged. She was a princess worthy of God.

The Nubian and Ethiopian women that were assigned to Mericah by the kings of their tribes and the Pharaoh back in Egypt, were promised an eternity of pleasure for themselves and the families of their homelands. In return they pledged themselves to live and die by her side.

Mericah, though she was of Ethiopian royalty, always treated the women around her as equals. She was known in Egypt as the fairest of all of Pharaoh's virgins. She was instinctively protective and feared no one.

Samo, her lifelong friend, was never far from her side. She loved and praised Mericah unconditionally. She had dedicated her life to serving the princess, which made her a very special woman, both on earth and into the heaven for kings.

Samo would not trade her life of serving Mericah for anything known to mankind. She felt as if she was a part of Mericah. In return, Mericah confided in her and thanked her daily for being there for her.

Chapter 33

Sa-hue was the captain of Mericah's ship, and he was the reason there was enough food. He and his men were fishermen with great skills, and made sure there was always plenty to eat. Drinking water was the real issue. The animal skin water containers were just about empty.

Sa-hue felt that they needed to reach land and find water with in the next ten days or they would be in trouble. He had hoped, by following the wind westward into uncharted waters, he would find solid ground. He thought he would be able to regroup and sail back eastward to the West Coast of Nubia and all would end well.

His lookouts searched for land from morning 'til night. They also watched the waters below for indications of land. For many days, they sailed on a voyage they had expected to last less than ten days. Even his own crew were getting weary and beginning to question Sa-hue's decision.

Rumors had been spreading that both ships were hopelessly lost and in the grasp of an evil god of Egypt. Word spread that Pharaoh had wished the princess to die at sea where the God of Moses had no domain. The knew that without Mericah, all of eternity would be lost to them.

Neither Mericah nor Mohab would permit anyone to pray to an idol or god of Egypt. If anyone was found praying to or worshipping the stone or metal gods of Egypt, they would be put to death and lose the status of eternal life.

The men and women began to refuse water in an effort to die for the princess and receive eternal life for themselves and the families in Nubia and Ethiopia. Five Ethiopians died from lack of water and their bodies were prepared and put into the sea. Four warriors on the second ship leaped into the sea to their deaths to assure more water for the princess.

"We must stop this madness and stop it now!" Mericah said, and demanded that the captain bring Mohab to speak to her.

Chapter 34

"All is not lost. We must not loose our faith and die without holding on," she said.

Mohab came to Mericah, and instead of the customary greeting of bowing his head as he approached, he hurriedly walked up to her and held her and hugged her to his chest. "I am so grateful that you have not been harmed."

She responded by cuddling against him with her eyes closed. After taking in a deep, relieving breath, she pushed herself back and spoke to her brother. "You must stop our people from refusing to drink."

"But they will not drink. No one on the second ship has taken water for two days. They want to move all of the remaining water to this ship so that you and the women and children may live. We have tried to force water into the mouths of some, but they waste it by spitting it out.

"This very morning, more than ten warriors leaped into the sea to give their lives for you. They have pledged to die for you. They think it is the most honorable way to receive everlasting life. They've wished and dreamed of dying in battle while taking you home. Now word has spread that to drink is to take the life of our princess. They will not drink."

"Stop them!" she demanded. "Tell them if they do not stop, I will leap into the sea and take my own life. There *is* hope. I know it has been hard and many have died; yet I know we will survive. Tell them they must drink. Land is near; I feel it in my soul.

"To die now is to give up when we have won our battle to live. Nemiah has died that we may live. I am sure that the God of Moses has received word that the evil of the sea has taken the life of the son of Moses. He will soon punish the sea and bring us home — all of us."

The women and children on the ship were listening and watching as Mericah threatened to take her own life if the sacrificial deaths continued. She walked to the ship's outer rail and held Ariah high above her head, as if to drop him into the sea.

"For the lives who are willing to die for me, I would gladly give up my child and then myself to this evil sea," she threatened. "The God of Moses has promised that we shall survive. He did not say it would be easy. He said it would be in a natural way, and though the evil gods have struck against us again and again and have taken the life of my child, I will not permit anyone to loose faith and give up their lives because of the lies and magical promises of the gods of Pharaoh.

"To die for me will not win an eternal life with the gods of Pharaoh in Egypt or anywhere in existence. The God of Moses is a living God. We must live right to gain favor and not die!" Mericah shouted.

She slowly brought Ariah back to her bosom. She said in a calm voice, "No one is going to die. We will live in the name of the God of Moses, just as He has intended."

Chapter 35

Night had fallen upon the two lost ships, and the rash of deaths had ceased.

Mericah was awakened by a female voice. "Mericah, I heard your heart crying out and I have come to comfort you."

"You have not come to comfort me, you have come to pity me and my people and I will not allow it!" Mericah said.

"That is what you are saying with your mouth but I have listened to your heart. I am here because you have brought me here," said the voice. "Don't let your pride invade the honesty of your heart. You are hurt, and rightfully so. You are confused and in need of God's assurance. I have come to assure you."

"Where were you while so many were dying and being swallowed by the sea? Where were you? I asked, when my child was ripped from my arms, but he was not saved. What can you assure me of? That you can only be near when you wish to babble about God, but not when you could save my boy? That you are here when you choose and not when you are needed? How can a god sit idly by while a child's life is swept away?"

Mericah began to weep while asking one last question. "Why wasn't He here?"

"Listen," responded the female voice, "God is always wherever you are. Natural occurrences of life are the rights of every living thing on earth. There would be no such thing as life for you if God interfered every time the nature of things reared up its head.

"If God decided every footstep for you, what would become of choice? What would become of making your own mistakes? What would become of lessons learned from going the wrong direction or being curious about the unknown?

"Is Nemiah dead or is Nemiah alive?" the voice continued. "What if your child fell from your grasp into the lap of God? Is this a bad thing or is it good? No one dies as an act of God. As you yourself have stated, God has given life. Where life goes will always be a mystery for mankind. If you have given life, would you let it be taken away meaninglessly?

"I am saying to you, let God mold the world, as it is His to mold. No life shall go away meaninglessly, for everything has a place in God's body. Whether a life is but a moment, a hundred or a million years, it becomes a part of the body of the life of God.

"How is it that you were willing to be sacrificed at the end of a Pharaoh's reign in exchange for an afterlife in a fictitious place where kings rule, and yet you fear that a life taken by God may just simply end?"

The voice was silent as Mericah pondered what had been said. The voice continued, "I know you are saddened by the loss of Nemiah. I, too, am saddened that you have lost a child so dear to you. I cannot question disastrous occurrences because I know God has not let Nemiah die and ... God's reasons are not as simple as yours and mine. Can you or I stop the life-ending things that occur? No, we cannot," she answered her own question.

"God has made us in a way that allow wounds to heal and the depths of pain are quickly forgotten. Memories, whether they are good or bad, will remain. We can let them haunt us and disrupt our lives or we can put them in a state of acceptance where they are beyond our ability to truthfully change."

"What does God want of me?" asked Mericah.

"What do you want?" the voice continued.

"I want to go home and live in peace with God," Mericah said.

"God has always been at peace with you, for in you He finds favor. It will not be long. You will soon find home. Life will never be easy in the eyes of those who see misery in every act of nature. I say to you, stay strong and your strength will be passed on for generations to come. Nothing can weaken you but self-distress. Your understanding of the will of God will grow as you grow. Yield not to the temptation to curse your God Almighty, for He will always and forever be there for you.

Chapter 36

"**L**and! I see land!" shouted the lookout of the lead ship. Everyone on the ship immediately turned his attention to the direction the ship was sailing, trying to see just what the lookout had spotted. Finally, there on the horizon was a massive coastline.

As they sailed closer, a shoreline of brown sand with huge green, vine-loaded trees came into view. Closer and closer they sailed. At captain Sa-hue's command, both ships turned parallel to the shore and began to sail southward. The captain was looking for an opening where he could safely anchor the ships.

After a short while, they entered into a natural harbor that was hidden behind a sand covered island. Both ships quietly sailed into the harbor and let down their anchors. Three men swam ashore. As they disembarked, Mohab directed twenty archers to build perches up in the highest trees to be used as lookout posts as well as battle positions.

Captain Sa-hue had his ships turn around to face the open sea in case there was an encounter of any kind. The remaining warriors came ashore and began building shelters. The women and children, including Mericah, were instructed to stay aboard the ship until the shelters were completed and the area was deemed safe.

Within three hours, a small fresh water stream was located and hunters brought back small game. "What are these animals?" Mohab asked while looking at one of the monkey-like animals.

"I don't know, we found them hidden in the base of trees. Some of the others we dug out of burrows in the ground," the warrior answered. "We haven't found any large game yet, but the others are still hunting. There are trees and bushes with fruit, but they are like none we have ever seen before."

The following day Mohab examined all the food that was gathered. Everyone was puzzled by the strange looking items. "Even the birds are like none I have seen before," said Mohab. "Cook the meatsand send it to the ships. Someone must test the fruit to make sure it is not poisonous before we distribute it."

After several days, the safe fruits were identified and sent aboard the ships. The scouts had begun reporting each day, and all of the reports were similar. They had not seen any humans and they had yet to see an animal they recognized. They hadn't found any horses, sheep, goats or big wild game of any kind.

For eight days, they journeyed in-land and still the scouts reported seeing no humans, but they did capture several larger animals that were frail, harmless, and had no pointed teeth.

Finally, Mohab instructed the women and children to come ashore. There was no immediate danger and no enemy to be found.

Months passed without a single encounter with another human. The scouts had gone as far away as two days running in every direction, looking for signs of an enemy, but found none.

Captain Sa-hue sailed along the coastline for ten days going north and then ten days going south, with scouts going ashore each day and they saw no one, no tracks, no campsites, not a trace of man.

Chapter 37

Three years had past since they stepped foot on this strange but friendly land. The scouts still journeyed southwest and north by land, while the ships journeyed north and south along the shore, setting up permanent camps. They reported each month that there was no change. There simply was no one else to find.

The warriors had put down their swords, and the archers used the tree perches to spot small game for the hunters. Surprisingly, they had stumbled into a land of plenty. The women began choosing mates and building huts for their new and expected families.

In the three years, their population had grown by nearly four hundred. There had been no deaths and the oldest person was no more than thirty years of age.

Animal oils and leather goods were becoming plentiful, along with an abundance of natural food and water. The weather was usually warm, with only a few months each year requiring the building of fires to keep warm through the night.

The women used their traditional abilities to weave clothing from small animal hides and plant fibers, while using berry juices and tree bark to add color and scent. They quickly discovered new techniques to make pot-like containers by heating red clay. They even discovered, accidentally, that by keeping fires burning for long periods, they could melt the sand. Once the sand cooled, it became a hardened substance that could be used for cutting rods. Shells from the sea were used for adornments and made music when blown into.

Mericah declared that ceremonies would take place to establish a permanent bond between chosen mates.

Mericah was now, at best record, about twenty-two years of age and her son Ariah was now six. Mohab spent less time guarding Mericah and more time pursuing Tamia, who was now carrying his third child.

With the population growing almost weekly; this small portion of land was nearly a perfect place to live. Even so, Mericah felt that her calling was still to reach the homeland and to take her position as queen. She still felt an urgency to introduce her people to the God of Mosses and to inspire them to worship and place their lives into the hands of the invisible, living God.

"Mohab," she said, "we have been here for more than three years. I think it's time I continue my journey to our homeland."

"Why?" asked Mohab.

"Because it is my destiny," she said.

"This is our destiny, right here. Here there is no bloodshed. There are no gods. This is where the God of Moses has led us. This you have said yourself. Why can't we stay here and live in the shadows of God?" asked Mohab.

"Yes," she said, "you should stay here with our people and my son. You should stay under the cloak of our God. You deserve all the happiness that God can bestow. You and Tarnia are strong, and even though she is Hebrew, your bond with her was made in the heavens. I, on the other hand," she said as she paused for a moment while looking out to sea, "I must deliver a message from God to our people back home."

"Please sister, stay here with us. Let God deliver the message. He can show the people the way, you cannot."

Mericah said, "They will not listen to men such as Moses, for they are set in their ways. I will tell our father of the non-existence of the stone gods and we will take God into Egypt and on to meet Moses at the Promised Land. We will give all of the northern lands back to the Ethiopians.

"Think of it Mohab, all of Ethiopoia, Nubia, Egypt and the land of the tribes of Israel, all under the reign of God and Moses. I would be queen of all the world. We will live by the laws of the God of Moses with all of His powers. Life will then be eternal with God right here on earth. I have seen his power, I have felt His power, I have heard His voice and I have felt His love.

"I don't know where we are, but I know we cannot be far from western Nubia. Sa-hue has said he believes we are on a huge island west of Nubia. This perfect place will be a part of our new world under God. The real God, my brother."

Mohab did not speak right away. He gave thought to what Mericah said as she stood patiently waiting for his response. "I will go with you," he said.

"No," she said, "you belong here. When I return, you will be here to welcome me. This will be the center of our homeland. In this place, we will build temples for the God of Moses, greater than the pyramids of Egypt. These temples will not be made of blood and stone. These temples will be built of dreams, under the direction of God. We will build as long as God is pleased. We will build places of learning and dwellings for kings and queens to come for thousands of years. The poorest of our people will live in homes built better than the palaces of the rich."

"How do you know these things?" asked Mohab.

"The female voice has showed me in a dream. I have seen the temples that reach into the sky. I have seen the powers of God who will bring pieces of the sun to earth. I have seen chariots without horses and thousands upon thousands of our people living in huts made of bricks that are like mansions of this day. How else can I bring the God of Moses here to show Him this new place we have found"?

Mohab listened but he was puzzled by the wishful talk of his sister. He could not understand how they could build such temples, even with the help of God. *My sister has lost her mind; there are no bricks here. Here there are only trees, plants and sand. Here there are no mountains from which to carve stone. There are not enough people or horses to apply the necessary might to move the stone even if it did exist here.*

"Don't worry," Mericah said. "All will be well. You shall see."

"I will send our best warriors with you and most of the gold and skins we have. That way, you can trade for passage home," Mohab said. "Has Sa-hue agreed to take you back? He worships you and will do anything for you, so I doubt it will be a problem. You will be safe with him and my warriors."

"He will take me back. He has been reading the stars. He believes the stars have changed positions. By his calculations, we are past the westward edge of the earth, which is impossible. If that were the case, we would have had fallen off the earth. He agrees. He has told me that the stars must have shifted because of the great storm we encountered while we were lost.

"The sun, he said, still rises in the east as it did every day we were at sea. So, it stands to reason, according to him, that we can catch the northwest wind and use the oars to get back to the mainland.

"We will need forty men and the Canaan crew. We will also need enough food and water to last at least the number of days it took to get here, which the captain believes should be about twenty. I know there are natural disasters that lie in wait for us, but I believe we can make it."

Chapter 38

One of the two ships was loaded and ready for the journey back home. During the time since they had arrived, Sa-hue had repaired and upgraded his ship and it was now more seaworthy than it had ever been.

There were forty Ethiopian warriors, twenty of the thirty-two Canaanites including Sa-hue, Mericah, three Nubian women and three Ethiopian women — a total of sixty-seven passengers. Sa-hue also loaded ten cages of live animals, nuts, dried fruits and plenty of fresh water. Two of the five remaining chests of gold and other items specially made for the trip would be used for trading. They were ready to embark.

Sailing toward home went just as Sa-hue predicted. Mericah spent most of her time talking to the six women and daydreaming about the future. When the winds died down, the men would work as oarsmen.

Sixty-one days had passed before the eastern horizon began to show shadows of land in the distance. They had not seen a hint of other ships or any indications of land during the entire journey. On the sixty-third day, they could smell the jungles of their homeland.

They sailed northeast along the shoreline until Sa-hue began to recognize some of the landmarks set at the end of the great sea to warn ships not to go any further. While sailing into the mouth of the great sea, Sa-hue approached Mericah with his shy mannerism leading the way. "We are in the western mouth of the great sea and soon we will be in waters we have chartered for fishing from the ports of Gaza," he said.

For the past three years or more they had essentially lived within yards from each other and they had never spoken about the Sa-Hue's homeland. The captain had truly thought he would never see home again.

Just like everyone else, he longed to see his family and friends, and like others, he had become both protective and spellbound by Mericah and her cause. It was to the point that his life only had meaning if she realized her destiny.

"Who are the Canaanites?" Mericah asked.

"We are the descendants of Canaan, who long ago settled east of Egypt in a place we call Gaza and northward along the coast of the great sea called Canaan," Sa-hue explained.

"Who is Canaan?" Mericah asked.

"It is said that Canaan was the grandson of Noah, who was the survivor of the greatest flood ever to happen to the world. I don't know the truth of the story, but Canaan was supposedly cursed by Noah because Canaan's father, Ham, took advantage of his stepmother after she had drunk fermented grapes. She later bore a child who was called Canaan.

"Noah was so angry that he cursed all of the children of Ham to be servants to the children of Ham's brother's descendants. As they grew older, Canaan and his brothers Cush, Mizraim and Put refused to serve. The sons of Ham fled southward along the coast of the sea, where they settled and created their own deities.

"Canaan, the father of the Canaanites, settled in what is now called the Kingdom of Canaan which is as far south as Gaza, and up to the southern borders of the Philistine. It is said that Cush, father of the great and mighty Ethiopian warrior called Nimrod, settled in the desert land of Nubia and Ethiopia, where their descendants developed a beautiful darker brown skin, such as yours. Thus, you and I could be of the same blood line of Ham, the son of Noah," Sahue explained.

"Why is it that I have never heard of the Canaanite?" asked Mericah.

"I cannot answer that, but I can tell you that Canaanites have traded with their southern brothers of Ethiopia for hundreds of years. It is said that the original people of Ethiopia did not suffer the floods of Noah. The Ethiopians are older than even the ancestors of Noah; their race of people extend from sea to sea in every direction south of Egypt, and have existed since time began.

"When I was a small boy, my father used to say to me, Sa-hue, there are many kinds of people on earth and they will be before you in many shapes, heights and colors. There will be none more trustworthy than the black people of Ethiopia. They do not have or need any gods, for God Himself has blessed them with inner peace and tranquility. He has protected them from the god of greed and the god of jealousy. In our day, it seems, they too have fallen prey to gods of Egypt," Sahue continued.

"Do the Canaanites know the God of Moses?" she asked.

"Yes," Sahue responded. "Once a man called Abraham lived in our land. He worshiped and praised the living God, but our people chose to trust in the god of Baal. It is said that God sent Abraham away from the land of Canaan and into Egypt. Since that time, the people have lost reason for self-discipline and self-rule.

"For hundreds of years they accepted and discarded many gods, even to a point where some animals, which had never been seen, were and still are worshiped by many of the tribes. Some of the kings called upon these animal gods to rule their kingdoms, leaving many to wonder if the sanity of our kings had not been stolen by Baal.

"It was believed, by some, that when Abraham departed, he took with him the only true God. The living God had not been heard from again until your people began to tell the stories of Moses and the exodus from Egypt with the help of the God of Abraham," Sa-hue said.

"Have you worshiped the gods of Egypt?" asked Mericah.

"No," Sahue answered. "My father and his father's father were fishermen. I have often heard my father curse the gods of the seas when our nets failed to retrieve a catch, but other than that I have always been taught that the gods of the land have no powers over the sea.

"That is why everyone was astonished when the stories were told of the dividing of the Red Sea to aid the exodus of the Israelites. We wondered about the majestic powers that He had over even the sea. Between the new stories of this God of Moses and the Israelites and the tales of the Ethiopian princess among us, there was more excitement in our land than there had been for hundreds of years," responded Sa-hue.

"When we are ashore, will you go with us and help me find Moses on our way to the homeland?" Mericah asked. "You will be rewarded greatly," she added.

"I would want nothing more than to go with you, but we have been gone nearly four years on a journey that was supposed to have taken days. My family probably has assumed my death. I can only imagine the joy of my return.

"The gold that you have given me is enough to make my entire village rich. More than likely I would not be welcomed in your land and I certainly would not be welcomed into the lands we must pass through to reach northern Nubia," Sahue said.

"Then I shall greatly miss your presence," she said. "I wish you and your men a full and prosperous life. Maybe some day we will meet again. Until that day, I will carry you in my prayers and God will bless you and yours."

Chapter 39

A fter a nearly four-year absence, the ship of the Canaan anchored on the shore of Gaza. The people of the village recognized a son of Canaan who had been rumored t o be dead at sea and who had now returned home. The ship was roped and pulled to the shore.

"At last I am home!'" Sahue shouted. With a proud grin, he came into the midst of his people, bursting with pride and eager to tell the stories of his survival. As he approached the familiar face of a neighbor of his childhood, he was greeted with a look of sadness.

Sahue said, "Greetings, my friend," while embracing the man with a hardy hug and pat on the back.

"Greetings," the man responded.

"Are my family members in the village today?" Sa-hue asked.

"No," he answered. Sa-hue began to realize that something was wrong by the expression on the friend's face. "No my friend, they are not here," he answered and then pulled Sa-hue away from the crowd. "I have sad news for you. You must leave here quickly. You and your men are in extreme danger."

"Why? Where are my parents and my brothers?" Sahue asked. "What is the danger? What has happened here?"

Several older women within hearing distance began to weep while pointing at Sa-hue. Others began to comfort Sa-hue's men as hey gathered around them.

"What has happened here?" Sa-hue asked again. His attention was drawn to one of his men's screams.

"No, No, this cannot be true! He cried.

"What has happened here? Tell me now!" Sa-hue said.

"The king," he sputtered as he continued for fear that Sa-hue would have the Ethiopian warriors kill him as the messenger of bad news, "the king has murdered your family and the families of your men," he said.

"Why? Why has he done this?" asked Sa-hue. "Tell me!"

"After you and your men left on your journey, the king decided that the gold he was given was not enough. Your father and the others refused to give up their share of the gold they were paid for the use of the ships and your crew.

"The next day, the king sent some of the Canaan soldiers to take it from them. While they argued back and forth, one of the solders drew his sword and sliced the arm of Ismael. Your father, seeing this, disarmed the soldier and slew him with his own sword. The rest of the villagers attacked the fleeing soldiers and drove them away.

"The following day, many soldiers returned and tortured one villager after another until they identified your father and the others. They searched their homes and yards until they found the Ethiopian gold. Before leaving, they tied the men, women and children to posts and their archers put them all to death," his friend said while sobbing from the horrifying memory.

"The king later declared that the god of Baa! ordered their deaths and yours. After spreading the word that Baal's men had overtaken your ship and slew the Ethiopian princess at the request of the Egyptian Pharaoh, we tried to fight back but we are fishermen. We were no match for the trained soldiers.

"Sa-hue, we loved your family and the others. The king has gone crazy with worry that Moses and the God of Abraham will return to punish him and the gods that they left behind. He has gathered every man of fighting age to destroy Moses. He has become cruel and ruthless and he will surely kill you out of fear of retaliation."

Sa-hue, a soft and gentle man of the sea, was stunned. As he stood motionless at the center of the crowd of people, everyone was silent and watched as Sa-hue and his men wept and cursed the king and the god of Baal.

Seeing the commotion, Mericah became concerned for her friend. She sent the Ethiopian warriors into the crowd with swords drawn to see what was upsetting the villagers. Sa-hue came back down to the shore to where Mericah had not yet left the safety of the ship. As he walked toward her at a hurried pace, she knew something had happened.

"What is wrong?" she asked. "Why are you crying?"

"I am angered and sickened, for the king has murdered our families," he said while shaking is head from side to side in grief.

Mericah gestured him to come to her. With both arms opened she embraced Sa-hue like a child as he wept uncontrollably.

"They have taken my family. What have I to live for? What is left for me?" he asked while still weeping loudly.

"They are not dead," she said. "They are the reason for you to live, for it will be you who shall win their presence before the God of Moses. You are alive and in you they shall live without threat of death at the hands of any man or god."

While Mericah stood quietly holding Sa-hue, a young Canaanite ran towards them. "Sa-hue!" he called out as two of the Ethiopian warriors grabbed him and held him. "Sahue, I am Tye!" he shouted. "I have news for you."

"Wait," said Sa-hue, "Bring him to here."

The two Ethiopians reluctantly brought him to Sa-hue and the princess. "What news have you?" he asked.

"Get off of me," the brave youth said while twisting his body out of the grasp of the warriors.

"Abram is not dead," he said. Abram was Sa-hue's youngest brother. "He is not dead, he is hidden southwest of here, toward the river of Jordan. He is with the giant people."

Sa-hue was rejuvenated by the news that at least his younger brother had survived. He turned to Mericah and asked, "Do you still want us to join you on your quest?"

"Yes," she answered. "You and any of your people who wish to join us are welcome."

Chapter 40

Searching for Moses

As the newly formed caravan traveled toward the River Jordan to find Sa-hue's brother, they gathered several hundred countrymen who were scattered throughout the valley. When they reached the land of giants, they were informed that Moses had led the Israelites north toward the Dead Sea, and they were warring with most of the nations along the way. While Israel conquered nation after nation in its' quest for the Promised Land, the Egyptians were fighting to survive the scorn of Nubia and her allies to the south.

Mericah wanted to see Moses once more before heading into the embattled land of Nubia on her journey toward home. Ten warriors rode just ahead of her, and there were four at her side and twelve about one hundred yards behind them.

In the jungles, twenty of these warriors could easily defeat two hundred of the enemy. They were well known throughout the world for their rhythmic moves as swordsmen, their accuracy with spears and their stamina and endurance. The Northlanders were known to jest that Nubians and Ethiopians could see their own ears, thus allowing them to spot their opponents as they approach.

In the mountain villages of Ethiopia, the favorite chore of young boys was to run messages from family to family through the bush. When Mohab was a boy, he was afraid of snakes. When it was his turn to run, he ran faster than anyone, while looking under nearly every bush in fear. As an adult, he developed the skill to advance toward a foe while being aware of bushwhackers, making him a most feared swordsman, even against more than one enemy at the same time.

In the late evening, they entered one of the outer campsites of the Israelites. Mericah's escorts pulled back and stationed themselves just out of sight but close enough to come to her aid if needed.

"I am Mericah," she said, identifying herself to the Israeli guards as she came within shouting distance. "I am the wife of Moses and I have come at his request." As she entered the campsite of the Levites, she realized they were aware of her level of importance because they immediately welcomed her and sent word to Moses that she was there.

After one day, Moses came anxiously to the love of his life. The last four years had taken their toll on his appearance. He wore the face of a man who has carried the weight of a nation. His hair and beard were bright silver against his bronzed, leather-like face. His eyes were set deep into his face where only the dark of his wide open pupils were visible; even so his eyes sparkled with glee as he walked majestically towards her. He reached for her hands t and brought them up to his chest.

Mericah stood mesmerized by the mere sight of the man she had longed for in her nightly dreams since the day they parted. He pulled her hands up to his lips, and gently kissed them, then nuzzled his face against them.

"I thought I would never see you again," he said softly. "Don't say a word, just let me hold you for a moment. Let me smell your hair so I may breathe again."

They embraced without speaking, until Mericah broke the long silence. "I know you said we would never see each other again on this earth, but I needed to be in your presence just once more. I have longed to stand by your side as you faced the onslaught of the world against you. I have prayed every day that God would reconsider and put our two nations together in route to the land of promise. I want desperately to be near you," she said.

Moses just stood there, holding her with his eyes closed. He seemed to be gathering her into his soul for himself and his God. Without a single word he was robbing her of her beauty, charisma and affection. She began to weaken from the strong and sudden drain on her love.

Mericah stood limply with her arms hanging at her side. The arms of Moses were the only reason she did not fall helplessly to the ground.

"Please," she weakly whispered, "Please stop or you will drain me of life."

Moses continued clinging to her not realizing he might be causing her serious harm.

"Please," she faintly repeated, "Please stop, you are killing me." Mericah knew that the magic of her heart could be taken from her by touch, but she never realized how much this godly man needed her to rekindle his strength. He had been drained by the commands of God and the needs of his people. Now, in the few moments that she was in his arms, he had taken her near to death without knowing it.

"Stop," she said, hardly able to breathe.

"Stop!" said the voice of the female angel of God who was suddenly standing near Mericah. "Let her go!"

Moses suddenly realized that he had nearly killed his love. He pulled himself away from Mericah, and held her up her now completely limp body. "I'm sorry! I did not know I was hurting you. I'm so sorry," he repeated while putting her gently onto the ground.

"She is all right," the angel said. "You nearly took her life. She is much too delicate to be used in that manner, but she is so willing to give her love to you and to God that she cannot stop herself. There is no other woman in this world capable of giving so much love as she. Her love is so pure that she cannot give it in abundance as other humans can. God, Himself, has marveled at the magic of her soul."

"Is she all right?" Moses asked, "I would never harm her. It's just that I was so overwhelmed with desire," he said.

"Yes, she will be fine," the angel answered.

"Who are you?" Moses asked in a humble voice.

The female angel hesitated as she looked down at Mericah, who was just beginning to regain consciousness.

"I am Eve, of whom you have written. I am also Mericah, who you love, and Mary, who will be. To you Moses, I am many, all of whom are of God. To her, I am just a voice that has been with her since childhood. She is as rare as an error of God. Of all the blessings that have come from above, she stands alone. I will never be far from her."

Mericah sat upright and put her exhausted head on Moses' shoulder. "I always seem to pass into a deep sleep when I am with you," she said.

Moses gathered her into his arms carefully as they both went off to sleep.

The following morning Mericah told Moses where she had been and what had happened to Nemiah during her four-year journey back to him. She knew she could not stay long, for both she and Moses were still obligated to their separate destinies.

Chapter 41

For three days, Moses continually taught her the wishes of the God of Israel. In those three days, she again was with child, or it should be said with children because she would bear her second set of twins. The boy, she would name Nerniah to honor her lost son, and a girl, Zernira.

Moses asked Mericah to take her people back to the new land where there was safety and peace. Moses knew that God had no boundaries on earth or in the heavens. "God shall be with you wherever you are, for He is the living God of the inhabitants of all the earth including the seas and the heavens above. Take with you all who wish to go from the tribe of Dinah, the daughter of Jacob.

"I wish to go first to see my father in the homeland," Mericah said.

"Your father and his armies are on the western side of the Red Sea, not far from where we crossed. You can go to your father's people, then northward to the sea from which you came. As for the Caananites and their allies, the nation of Israel, under the direction of God, shall pass judgment upon them with a vengeance. The Caananites have ignored the demands of God and have not respected the resting place of Abraham."

Most of the Hebrew tribe of Dinah joined Mericah on her journey. Abram and Sa-hue were pleased to hear that Moses and the Israelites would avenge their family that had been murdered by the king of the Caananites.

Fifteen days after her departure, Mericah returned to the valley of the river Egypt. Once there, they prepared to advance to the West Bank of the Red Sea to meet her father. Fifteen thousand tribesmen, women and children joined Mericah at the river to journey to the new lands as instructed by God through the word of Moses.

After thirty days of travel westward, the tribe, including Mericah's people, came face to face with a regiment of the Pharaoh's armies. The Egyptian regiment was badly battered and appeared to be retreating.

Mericah and the Hebrew tribe of Dinah had inadvertently cut off the Egyptian retreat with the Nubians and Ethiopians in pursuit. The Egyptians were no match for the battle ready Hebrews, who had the support of Mohab's best tactical warriors. Within hours, the Egyptians were cut down.

As the Nubian and Ethiopian armies advanced, finding the armies they had pursued lying destroyed along the sea, they paused to observe this new unfamiliar army that stood before them. The black men stood shoulder to shoulder in preparation to carry on their advance. They were not sure how to approach this unidentified mass of armed men.

Both armies faced off for battle as Mericah received word of the confrontation by an army of black men. The army of blacks began to hum loudly, and the humming sound filled the area for miles. It sounded as if all the bees on earth had lowered the tone of their buzz and amplified the sound a thousand times.

The brave men of Mericah's army were unnerved by this strange noise made by the black men. The humming suddenly stopped, then thousands of soldiers pounded their shields against their spears to create a loud clapping sound, which was twice as loud as the humming.

A colorfully dressed horseman raced towards Mericah's army and suddenly stopped and raised his arm to signal a full attack. During the short pause before the attack, the guardian warriors sent to protect

Mericah rode toward the colorfully dressed Nubian soldiers. Mericah's forty black Guardian warriors dismounted and formed a wall, standing shoulder to shoulder, as thousands of enemy soldiers quietly looked on.

The Guardians pulled down their protective masks and readied themselves for battle. The signaling Nubian soldier lifted himself high above his horse's back and then sat down again. He slapped his legs against the sides of his horse and rode bravely toward the Ethiopian guardians.

He turned his horse sideways as he continued to slowly approach the guardians. He seemed puzzled by the foolish courage of the battle-ready guardians. He still hesitated to signal the attack. Mericah's army stood ready to fight.

Without warning Mericah rode out into the open, dressed in the Ethiopian garb she had kept with her over the years. Oh, what a sight she was for the angels of God to see. Mericah was sitting so proud, so beautiful, and so brave before the thousands of soldiers of her own birth nation.

Closer and closer she came toward the Nubian horseman. He turned toward the approaching princess and sat still, waiting for her with his sword drawn at his thigh. Mericah rode up to the soldier and paused as the horse she was riding pranced in place. She removed the silk scarf covering her face revealing a gold ornament hanging on her forehead that had been given to her by her father.

The Nubian soldier looked directly at Mericah. His horse reared up as he slapped his legs against its sides. He pulled the reins and dashed toward his own armies with his sword still in hand. A ranking officer of the Nubians overlooking the strange event came to the front line and met the galloping horseman as he approached. They spoke briefly and the officer motioned to two others within the ranks. The soldiers quickly come forward and the three of them rode swiftly out to Mericah.

"Who are you?" one of the men asked.

"Mericah," she answered. The three turned and rode back towards the waiting armies. They went off in three different directions, yelling loudly as they approached other officers moving forward from the ranks.

Then, the army of men began to lay down their shields and swords. One after the other they bowed down, putting their faces to the ground.

Oh, what a marvelous sight all the angels of the heavens paused to view. Within minutes, wave after wave of men fell; first to their knees and then bending down until their faces touched the ground.

Mericah bravely rode closer, slowly with her head held high. Instinctively, she arched her back and raised her chin as she continued along the front lines of the opposing army.

Twenty or so horsemen rode toward her from the distance. They were dressed like kings instead of soldiers. As they came closer, she saw them divide to make way for one huge man whose horse was laden with gold and adornments. She recalled that her father had dressed this way for special ceremonies when she was a child.

The huge man stopped just short of reaching Mericah. He removed his headdress and looked directly into her eyes. Throughout the battle zone there wasn't a sound, even the horses stood motionless and silent. The man dismounted and walked up to Mericah's horse. She looked directly at him with her chin still held high. She took a deep breath as if to speak but she said nothing. The man walked from one side of her to the other, gazing into her eyes. She followed his movement with her eyes.

"Mericah," the deep voice said.

She was startled, as the voice sounded like Mohab's. She quickly lowered her chin and looked into the face of this man who sounded like her brother.

"Who are you?" she asked.

The man cocked his head to one side. He, too, sensed a familiar tone in her voice. After a few moments of exchanging puzzled looks, Mericah spoke again. "I asked, who are you?"

The man looked puzzled, but still did not answer. "Have you no tongue?" Mericah asked.

He slightly reared back his head as he realized the voice resembled that of the young sister he had left back in the city. "I am Raheed," he answered. "Who are you?"

She again was startled by the familiar voice. "Why do you have the voice of Mohab?" she asked.

"Mohab?" he said while instantly perking up. "How do you know my brother?"

"Your brother?" she asked.

"Yes, where is he?" he asked while gazing around at the men with Mericah. "Where is my brother?" He turned his back to Mericah, then took several steps with his hand covering his brow. He suddenly paused as he realized that he was talking to his oldest sister, whom he could not remember seeing before.

"For the sake of the gods, you are the princess. You are the one we have awaited! You are the one we have come to find for the sake of the gods," he said as he too knelt in front of her horse.

There were sounds of astonishment coming from the ranks as they watched the young king bow to the woman. She must truly be Mericah.

"Get up!" she demanded. "Where is my father?" she asked as she moved her horse a little closer, while looking into the distance for her father.

"Our father is dead. He was killed in battle," the young king said, "Our mother died of grief not long after. You are the queen of all the land," the young king declared as he again bowed to her.

Chapter 42

The would-be battle zone was suddenly friendly, and all the soldiers were put at ease. They celebrated the return of the queen and sent word throughout the land that she had come home.

The newly joined nations of Nubia, Ethiopia and the tribe of Dinah were encamped west of the Red Sea, just south of the heart of Egypt. The leaders called a meeting to determine how they were going to proceed. The question to be answered was whether they should continue northward and drive what was left of Egypt's armies into the great sea and reclaim all of Egypt for Nubia or return to Nubia and Ethiopia with their allies and live in peace under a new treaty and the new living God.

These and other options were brought to the table of decision. The leaders were not able to agree entirely, so they decided to take the choices to Mericah.

Mericah was told about her young sister, Kalah, who was destined to be queen if Mericah had not returned. She was told of their similarities and how the people had learned to love her and Mericah's younger brother, who had been acting as king in Mohab's place. Mericah summoned her younger sister and they met for the first time.

While this new nation was encamped in the Delta, awaiting her decision, Mericah spent three months teaching her brother and sister all she had learned about the God of Moses and the laws bestowed upon the Israelites. She instructed them to abandon the stone gods and replace them with the living and invisible God. She told them of the new land that their brother ruled. She told them of a day when they would again be joined with all of their ancestors through the grace of the living God.

Finally, she told them of her decision to go back to the new land far west of the great sea. There, she would join their brother and raise her son and the children she carried in her womb.

When the time came, Mericah was ready to bid farewell to her family and those of her people returning to the Ethiopian homeland. Before she left, she called a meeting with Sa-hue and his loyal Canaans, Sebah the leader of the Ethiopian warriors, four leaders from the Hebrew tribe of Dinah and the leaders of the Nubians.

After a full day of listening to all their concerns, she spoke as the queen she had become, "The Ethiopians have the choice of going home to the highlands of Ethiopia or going on with me to the new land. The tribe of Dinah is welcome to join me or you can go to Ethiopia."

To the Nubians who wanted to take back Egypt she said, "We will go with you all the way to the shores of the great sea and crush any Egyptian resistance that stands against the living God of Moses. However, we will not murder a single person who is willing to surrender, including the Pharaoh's men."

"My friend, Sa-hue and his people may join us in the new land, but if they do this, they must destroy all remnants of the gods of the Canaans and swear to abide by the laws given to Moses by God. They are imprinted into my heart and mind."

The things Mericah said were well understood, and the leaders disbanded the nations accordingly. Like a forest fire, the new tribe of Mericah and the Nubians swept north to the great sea with little resistance. They worked hard for six months, building and preparing existing Egyptian ships for the westward voyage.

In all, there were nearly twenty thousand people waiting to go with Mericah. According to Sa-hue, such a massive number of people would require at least fifty seaworthy ships. The fleeing Egyptian noblemen had taken most of the best ships. With just twenty ships available, it would take as many as three journeys round-trip journeys to carry all of the people to the new land.

Chapter 43

The Journey

Before the start of the journey, Mericah had an ark built of gold and precious jewels similar to that which Moses had built while the Hebrews were at Mt. Sinai. She had it built according to exact instructions from Moses. The Ethiopians placed the ark on the second ship of the convoy to protect the possessions of the ship. Mericah prayed to the God of Israel, just as Moses had done, and instructed that only the pure at heart should touch the ark.

The final count was forty ships of all different sizes that the men had managed to make seaworthy. Some were in good shape, others not so much. With glee and giving praise to God, the people boarded and filled every nook. The Nubians watched as the others loaded everything possible for the voyage to the new land.

"Mericah has prophesied that someday we shall board such ships and be taken to the new land of God, I can only hope that we, too, will glow with excitement when that time comes," said the Nubian leader.

Meriah knelt down as many watched and listened to her pray aloud to God. "All Mighty God, we are before you as subjects of your command. As far as our eyes can see, we are here with pleading hearts. Our eyes have been opened and we no longer recognize the carved stones of the Egyptians as gods to bow down to. We are about to embark upon a journey. We are taking ships filled with goods and hearts filled with hope. Most of all, we are carrying spirits filed with You, the living God of Abraham, Israel, Moses and the Hebrews. We are placing ourselves in Your hands that You may also be called the living God of hope. Hope for those who are not listed in your book of tribes.

Bless our journey and those who have stayed behind that we may find favor in Your heart and all of mankind can be called the children of God wherever they dwell, upon. Your earth as well as the heavens."

Chapter 44

The exodus included Mericah and all those who chose to follow her, including Sa-hue and all of the Canaanites who chose the God of Moses, Seba and all of the Nubians who chose to follow him, the tribe of Dinah, daughter of Israel, and all who chose to follow them. They also gained many along the way who had seen and felt the power of God. In all, the final census at sea was twelve thousand people, excluding the unborn.

When Mohab's lookouts spotted the many ships on the horizon, they did not know what to think. Mohab ordered his men to prepare for battle because they did not recognize the ships and there was no way to know if they were friendly. The ships were Egyptian and they were thought to be carrying the Pharaoh's armies.

Sa-hue, sensing that Mohab would not recognize them, had the ships anchor off shore while he brought his ship carrying Mericah into the familiar bay. As they came closer and closer to land without seeing a single soul, Sa-hue instructed his men to loudly identify themselves in the language of the Ethiopians.

"Mohab!" they yelled, "It is us, Mohab it is us. It is Mericah, Mohab!"

When the warriors heard the name of Mohab, they began to let themselves be seen. They waved and signaled inland that there was no danger. Sa-hue was relieved when Mohab finally carne into view.

"Greetings my brother, it is good to have you back," Mohab said with his familiar big wide grin.

"Who is with you? Who is aboard all of those ships?" he asked.

"Mericah is here," Sa-hue answered to Mohab's surprise. "The ships are filled with our people. God has blessed us with a safe journey, for not one life has been lost," he shouted as men began to tie ropes off and pull the ship to the shore.

"Mohab, I am here!" Mericah shouted, drawing his attention. "Greetings, my brother. We have returned to start the most godly journey of our nation and of the world."

Mohab jumped onto the ship and ran to his sister with opened arms. "I have worried and prayed many nights, hoping that you were safe and that we would see each other again."

"I, too, have worried and prayed," she said, "but, God has seen us through."

"Welcome home, my sister, our queen," replied Mohab.

It took three days to unload all the people and cargo from all of the ships. All but six of the ships were dismantled shortly thereafter and the materials were used to build shelters and the start of new villages.

Most of the tribe of Dinah located to the northwest of the main site, which was now a well-organized village. The Caanans, who were accustomed to the sea, located directly north along the waterway where the ships were stored for use in fishing and exploratory voyages. The Nubian tribes were moved south, while the Ethiopians and those already living in the village stayed in the center of the land at the mouth of the waterway.

With help from Sa-hue, Seba, and Abrarn, Mohab and Mericah established governing rules and appointed a council made up of leaders from each tribe or family that numbered more than fifty. In all, there were twenty-six council members with twenty-six different responsibilities, ranging from issues such as food distribution to sanitary areas used for human discharge.

Mohab was elected to settle all disputes. Anyone found guilty of breaking a council law would be put to sea or escorted past the furthest outpost to the west of the center village, along with his entire family. They were to be marked with ink and not permitted to return.

Public worship was not permitted. All prayers and worship were to be done by Mericah or her appointee only and without exception. Anyone caught in possession of an idol that represented a god would be put to death at sea, where he or she would remain dead forever.

Seba was selected to oversee all of the hunting. The use of weapons by anyone other than Seba's guardians was to be punished by cutting off the thumbs of the violators.

Sa-hue was in charge of all sea voyages for exploration and fishing. Abrarn was selected to oversee and to set values of trade and labor. He was also responsible for the storing and accounting of food for times of drought or other emergencies.

Each family elder of fifty tribesmen or more was appointed as chief and was made responsible for the order of authority within his own tribe.

Mericah was chosen, by God, as Queen and ruler of this new nation, hereafter called the nation of Mericah.

In the fall of the year 1240 B.C., Mericah bore her second set of twins Moses was unaware of his new descendants born thousands of miles away from his pursuit of the Promised Land.

After ten years, the nation of Mericah grew to more than sixty thousand. There was no way to continue taking census accurately with that many people. The explored territory grew by hundreds of miles in every direction, without a single sighting of a single human other than their countrymen.

There was virtually no sickness. Deaths were from old age or accident. In the ten-year span, there were sixteen deaths and thousands of births.

Peace was a way of life and war revealed itself as an unreasonable solution. Men were admired for their creativity and successful hunting or fishing.

Without having to cater to false gods, men were able to spend more time giving praise to the achievements of their fellow men, women and children. Mericah permitted the people to give thanks to God by sharing their bounty with their neighbors.

The greatest men were recognized by the number of gifts they bestowed upon friends and strangers. The people began to believe that God awarded kindness with success and ability. The gods of Egypt were finally dead and the stage had been set for a new beginning...

"Many years have come and gone since the day we arrived," Mohab said to Mericah and the council. "There are hundreds of villages along the coast and inland for many, many miles now. We have been blessed with peace and an abundance and good health. The council members now number more than one hundred and that number is growing each year as our people spread and multiply throughout the land.

"Our scouts have journeyed far and have set up new village sites hundreds of miles in every direction. We have yet to encounter any other nation. On clear days we have learned to signal by smoke from fires and by relaying by word of mouth from village to village, but we have had no news of an enemy."

Chapter 45

In your mind, imagine a place where the land is warm and gentle, where the earth is rich with plant life and the sea abundantly filled, where animals are submissive to mankind. Where the air is pure and filled with the music of the lark, robin, and sparrow. Where the days are bright with sweetness in the air, come rain or come shine. The nights come quietly bringing a view of the universe and leaving with a view of the rising sun peering over the distorted midst of the sea.

Imagine a nation of people, people with warm smiles of joy, and no tears of fear.

Imagine a group of young boys trying to leap the distance of a small stream or giving chase to a wild turkey that they can't possibly catch.

Imagine a group of young girls searching the shoreline or beds of flowers, gathering objects of beauty for the art and games of adornment.

Imagine an old man, who is anxious to move on to his own place of promise, telling stories of his childhood and how things used to be in a matter of fact way.

Imagine men constantly building the new and tearing down the old, enhancing their skills to win the respect of their comrades or the admiration of fine-looking women.

Imagine a woman ... cradling a newborn against her breast or another sharing a romantic story of a young man who has finally taken notice. He has suddenly stopped jumping streams or chasing birds he cannot catch, or another who has learned the pleasures of the art of braiding, coloring pottery or designing colorful clothing.

Imagine Mericah, tall and slender, with blemish free skin, elegantly shaped legs, and brown skin that turns shades of gold under the sunlight. She seldom laughs out loud, yet she always seems to be slightly smiling. Her small breasts held high by her gently rounded shoulders and her towering neck. Her arms are sleek and her voice is often soft and filled with kindness until she becomes puzzled, when she lifts her chin and brings down her brow to deliver a voice that turns stern and confident, like that of a Queen.

Imagine a place where people have, by some miracle, found harmony. A place under leadership that sits well with those who are led. A leadership that, until called upon to lead, blends within its own environment.

Mericah demanded and was a part of such leadership under a God that did not disrupt for His own sake of praise or worship.

Chapter 46

One morning, Mericah awoke disturbed and with fear for the first time in many years. For ten nights she'd had a reoccurring dream. On the first night she dreamed of an Egyptian ship appearing off shore. Aboard the ship was God. He was staring at her with glowing red eyes of envy.

Without moving His lips He spoke to her, "I am Lord," he said in a loud earth-shaking voice. "I am called by the name of—"

Mericah awoke without hearing the name of the lord.

On the second night, the same ship appeared with God holding a brass lamp with seven candles. "I am God the Almighty, I am called by the narne of—

On the third night the ship was closer and God again appeared standing on board. He was dressed in a white robe and in His hand He held a cross. "I am called by the name of—"

On the fourth night He held a piece of the moon, on the fifth night a star. Each night God held a different object and yet made the same statement, "I am God."

Mericah kept repeating before she awoke, "I am called by the name of—"

On the tenth night, His eyes were no longer fiery red. His eyes, even from the distance, were covered with tears and reflected the flickering light of the stars. He calmly stepped off the ship and onto the surface of the sea. He slowly walked towards Mericah. In one hand was the branch of an olive tree, in the other was a stem of thorns. Under the hood of His robe, across His forehead was a thin twisted strip of cloth soaked and dripping with blood.

She envisioned in this tenth dream that each previous God had swiftly come ashore without saying His name.

On the tenth night, God approached her. He paused and said in a frightening voice, "I am your Almighty God. I am called by the name of names. I am the only God. You shall not call upon me to change what I have already written. Within my body, I alone possess all things throughout all time. Each time holds the spirits of millions of men. Each man shall change but none shall die. His time shall be sacred. He shall cling in vain until the day his eyes will be opened."

In this final dream, God ascended upward into the open doors of heaven, just as Mericah awakened. Mericah summoned Mohab and told him of her dreams of the last ten nights.

"What do you think it means?" he asked.

"I don't know. I have heard of men and women who interpret dreams but I cannot. I don't know if these dreams have meaning or if they are just unusual dreams. My heart is uneasy because of a feeling that I have that there is a meaning."

In the middle of the eleventh night, all ten dreams were accelerated and repeated again and again. Mericah awoke frightened by the swiftness of the visions and the loudness of the Lord's voice. In the darkness of night, she was startled to see the angel, Eve, standing at the foot of her bed.

"Your sense of fear has brought me here," the angel said. "What has caused your heart to beat with such alarm?"

"I am afraid," Mericah answered. "I have dreamed for ten nights that God has come here to reveal His name. Each time, I have awakened before He completes His words. Each night He has entered into our land as the same God with ten different names. In the last dream He spoke of the times for men. I could only listen without understanding," Mericah said.

"God is seldom His own prophet," said the angel. "For man has proven himself to be weak and unable to follow instructions. Every man's life is much too short. Men tend to take a look into the realm of God, only to see themselves as a small thread in a huge garment. Perhaps you, like many before you, have had visions of what you think is meaningful to God. Or perhaps you have been given a vision of what is to come," the angel said, "I do not know."

Mericah's instinctive ways overwhelmed her thoughts. She needed to know. She could not help but ask the angel, "Is it not true that where there is a god there is also disruption and confusion among the people?"

"It appears that way, but men create all types of gods to serve their personal needs. If a god does not conform to their thoughts they conjure up one who does. Frightened and confused people in search of fulfillment will believe in a false prophet if there is no other voice.

"Every man and woman will listen to the wind, hoping to hear an answer to the riddles of their own life. Without gods, you and your people have done very well in the eyes of the Lord. If you are wise, you will continue to take each day as it is presented to you. People should do what they were created to do according to the plan of God — to be fruitful and multiply upon the earth, to accept the gifts of God and to obey the laws that have first and foremost been instilled into the hearts of men to pursue righteousness and experience the joys of this life with God's blessings and according to the natural order of things.

Let the gods live according to the gods, and angels according to angels. For gods to live as men or men to live as gods is foolish — one has no knowledge of the other. You are wise to know that life according to God is far beyond the imagination of the wisest of men.

There is the life of the supreme God and His host of angels and there is a supreme life for mankind of which we strive to attain. There is everlasting turmoil when the boundaries are crossed through man's self-proclamation of knowing what God has in store," the angel Eve said.

Mericah seemed to understand. She had led her new nation according to the words of the angel, with the common sense of men, and the instincts given to her by God. Mericah's spirit of good was pleasing to God.

As Meriah lay alone on her deathbed, tears faintly streaming down each side of her face, she began to feel a presence she had not felt in all her days.

"Why are you crying?"

"Because I am afraid."

"Have you ever been afraid before?"

"Not such fear as this," she answered. '

'What are you afraid of?"

"Of dying," she said.

"Why are you afraid of death?"

"Because it is something I've never experienced before and I don't know if God loves me."

"I do. ... What does afraid feel like? I ask because I don't recall placing fear in the spirit or the heart or the mind of mankind. Yet, all who come to me are afraid."

"It feels like hopelessness. It feels like running along a high cliff with my eyes shut and not being able to open them, and not knowing how to stop. It feels like death is near. It causes me to pray," she said.

"Fear is not of me, it is the only evil that I cannot take from man or angel. So be it. Where is it that pains you?"

"It pains me in my heart and in the depths of my mind, in the place where my tears are stored. It pains as if my breath can only exhale until I am drained of consciousness and strength."

"Hold my hand, he said. "Is fear still within you?"

"No," she answered.

"Would you like to come home with Me?"

"Home to Ethiopia?" she asked.

"No, home with Me."

"Home to Moses in the Promised Land?" she asked.

"No ... Home with Me."

"Who are you?" she asked.

"I am God."

Mericah had no more questions. She simply closed her precious eyes and put her hand into his. Every heart stood still as God himself pulled her to his bosom. He had reclaimed what was rightfully His. She was the jewel of the Nile.

Mericah had lived one hundred and twenty-two years. After death, her body was placed on a wooden platform for two days. On the third day, her body was buried. The nation of Mericah survived for a thousand years, and was the only perfect living environment known to man. After one thousand years, the gods again found their way into the lives of men. With the gods came turmoil, evil and the need for the Almighty.

In 1922 A.D., a group of men digging near the shores of what is now South Carolina unearthed a nearly three thousand year old burial site. It was assumed to be the burial site of a certain tribe of Native Americans, and that it was...

About the Author

J ack Thomas Reynolds was born in a small coal mining town just outside of Pittsburgh, Pa., and is the father of six daughters. He has always loved art and the art of telling stories; his own and the stories of others he has come to know.

He says of himself, "I came up through the cracks at a time when a black man falling through cracks was very easy to achieve." He credits all of his positive achievements to the fact that he has always abstained from mind-altering substances — drugs, alcohol and tobacco. He blames his shortcomings on his own stubbornness. If he had a motto, it would be one of his friend's sayings: "There is nothing on earth stronger than love and comradeship."

www.ingramcontent.com/pod-product-compliance
Lightning Source LLC
Chambersburg PA
CBHW020524120726
47904CB00003B/965